W9-BCL-011

PRAISE FOR RUSSELL BANKS

"This gifted writer makes us care about the characters he creates."

Cultural Information Service

"Banks has a remarkable ability to let us observe a situation through the eyes of disparate characters and to convey their feelings with skill and compassion."

Newsday

"Banks' talent is capturing not simply events, words, and thoughts but, somehow, the density of molecules around his characters, the smell before, the being during, the taste afterward."

The Middletown, N.Y. Record

"Anything Banks writes is worth reading!"

The Raleigh, N.C. News and Observer

"Banks is a major talent."

Fort Lauderdale News and Sun Sentinel

FAMILY LIFE

Russell Banks

BALLANTINE BOOKS • NEW YORK

Portions of FAMILY LIFE have appeared in these periodicals: *Tri-Quarterly*, *Z-Z* and *Extreme Unctions and Other Last Rites* (Latitudes Press).

Copyright © 1974, 1975 by Russell Banks

All rights reserved under International and Pan-American Copyright Conventions, which includes the right to reproduce this book or portions thereof in any form whatsoever. Published in the United States of America by Ballantine Books, a division of Random House, Inc., New York, and simultaneously in Canada by Random House of Canada Limited, Toronto.

Originally published by Avon Books, a division of the Hearst Corporation in 1974.

Library of Congress Catalog Card Number: 75-725

ISBN 0-345-34693-9

Manufactured in the United States of America

First Ballantine Books Edition: June 1988

For Mary Gunst

"A poor prince who is weak in cavalry, and whose whole infantry does not exceed a single man, had best quit the field; and signalize himself in the cabinet, if he can get up into it—I say *up into it*—for there is no descending perpendicular amongst 'em with a *'Me voici! mes infants'*—here I am—whatever many may think."

LAURENCE STERNE,
A Sentimental Journey

Chapter 1

1.

TO GO BACK TO THE BEGINNING WOULD BE FRUITLESS, timewasting, pretentious. It's much more productive, faster and more sincere to commence *in medias res* with the king squealing angrily, the princes, all three of them, lolling through their extended adolescences, the queen quietly comforting herself in her chambers, and the several secondary characters gathered together in small groups scattered variously about the palace—the Green Man (so-called), the Loon, the Twit, Genghis, *etc., etc*.

This, then, is not unlike the opening scene of a favorite opera, *The Trojans,* by Hector Berlioz (after *The Aeneid,* by Virgil), Part 1, "The Sacking of Troy." That is, one thinks of that narrator, and of Cassandra, Coroebus, Andromache, Astynax, Aeneas, Priam, Hecuba, Panthus, Helenus, Ascanius, Polyxena, Hector's Ghost, and others (in order of appearance), and one thinks of Troy or Carthage or of a castle-like citadel inside a ravaged city, of city walls and a vast plain beyond, and one recalls that particular narrative line and obtains thereby a pretty fair idea of how it all begins.

2.

THIS IS INTENDED, ACTUALLY, TO BE A FAMILY STORY, after the Greeks. But after Thomas Wolfe, too. And Gertrude Stein. Certain late nineteenth-century Russian novelists. William Faulkner. Marcel Proust. Thomas Hardy. Henry James. D.H. Lawrence. New England poets of the mid-twentieth century. André Gide. The Scandinavian playwrights. Truman Capote. Wright Morris. Nathaniel Hawthorne. Vladimir Nabokov. John Milton. Philip Roth. George Bernard Shaw. Washington Irving. James Agee and Walker Evans. Charles Dickens. Harriet Beecher Stowe. Sigmund Freud. Eudora Welty. William Burroughs, Jr. Laurence Sterne. Thorstein Veblen. William Carlos Williams. Edna Ferber. The Grimm Brothers. William Saroyan. Anton Chekhov. William of Occam. James Branch Cabell. John Steinbeck. Ellen Glasgow. Sarah Orne Jewett. Frank Norris. Katherine Anne Porter. J. D. Salinger. Franz Kafka. Anne Frank. Sinclair Lewis. Bede. Erskine Caldwell. Charles Addams. Tennessee Williams. James T. Farrell. Rollo May. Giovanni Boccaccio. Theodore Dreiser. Elia Kazan. Sherwood Anderson. Henry Fielding. Louisa May Alcott. Zelda Fitzgerald. Oscar Handlin. Thornton Wilder. Flannery O'Connor. The King James Version of the Old Testament. William Makepeace Thackeray. Ed Sanders. Jane Austen. Ignazio Silone. Issac Bashevis Singer. Ernest Jones. And Ford Madox Ford. —After these, too.

After them in *time,* of course, if not in manner. Yet also, and perhaps more importantly than either time or manner, after them in a subtler way, and suggesting through that a previously unrecognized, yet ancient tradition, the nature of which should be apparent as soon as one has considered which authors, insofar as their names are absent above, cannot be said to participate in that tradition: The Tradition of the Bloody Orange.

3.

The Tradition of the Bloody Orange—
A Paradigm

SOMEONE APPEARS ON THE HORIZON AS A BLACK SPECK, a fly stuck against the lavender sky. He draws closer and closer, at first slowly and then more rapidly, until he has drawn face-to-face with the viewer, whereat he is repelled. He tries not to reveal the depth and extent of his revulsion, nausea, disgust, boredom, by describing himself, his family, his friends and lovers, and the enemies of all. At last, unable to conceal his true feelings any longer, he draws from the leather pouch at his waist a large Florida orange (of the hybrid type, called "navel"). He brings the perfect sphere slowly up to his mouth, which is ample, and chomps suddenly into it, splattering billows of blood over his face, hands, green lamé shirt and tan suede boots. Then, continuing to eat at the orange, he turns and withdraws quickly to the horizon again, where he remains, a speck of changing color from black to red to orange and sometimes (to the naked eye) appearing cadmium yellow or even, as he should, green. From such a distance, he is quite beautiful to observe, changing color like that, especially against the lavender sky!

4.

THIS IS THE START OF THE ACTION. A HANDSOME YOUTH who wore slick green suits and strangely decorated hats went to the king with three sons and expressed in public a passionate desire to have one of the sons for his lover.

—I don't care which one, he cried. —Any of them will satisfy me. I have this thing about princes, he said.

5.

FOR TWO DAYS AND NIGHTS, THE KING AMBLED DOWN the many-tapestried corridors of the palace, laughing and murmuring to himself. —A thing about princes, indeed. That's rich!

6.

IT WAS A LATE, AMBER-COLORED AFTERNOON. IN THE gymnasium the three princes practiced the sports. Naked and oiled, they ran and kicked and threw. Soft light from the windows above drifted down and shimmered over their sleek bodies.

One of the ballboys attending them, a cripple desperately seeking favor and possible advancement, told them about the young man in the slick green suit and his strange request. The way the ballboy told it, the man's request was actually a demand, ominously put.

—He gave your father, His Royal Highness the King,

6

just three days to decide which one it would be, the ballboy told the athletes.

They laughed and called the ballboy a twit. —Far out, twit! they teased.

7.

IN DEFENSE OF HIMSELF, THE BALLBOY CHANGED HIS story and said that he'd made up the part about the funny-looking hat with the geraniums in it and the tan suede boots and the moustache and even the accent with all the flat A's. But it availed him nothing. The princes pelted him with handballs, badminton birdies, medicine balls, and basketballs. They even fell to rolling a shot put at his feet, aiming for the arches. They were disturbed.

8.

THE KING FUCKED THE QUEEN ON TWO SUCCESSIVE nights, keeping the lights on throughout copulation on both occasions. He was obviously disturbed.

9.

—I LIKE A PLUCKY FAGGOT, HE BREATHLESSLY CONFIDED to the queen after each of her orgasms. After his own, however, he remained silent.

10.

THE QUEEN, PONDERING BOTH HIS REMARK AND THE TIMing of his silences, had difficulty sleeping. At breakfast following their second night of love, she asked her husband, —Have you ever performed a sex act with a man? Or with a boy?

—My dear, he answered.—I once caught and screwed a loon. Unforgettable! Jesus, I had an appetite! he bellowed, heading swiftly for court.

11.

THE THREE PRINCES WERE ALREADY THERE, WAITING NERvously for him to arrive. They wanted to know beforehand how the king was going to handle this one. In this matter, they each had a private ambition for the king's policy. The oldest son was named Orgone. He was a well-known wrestler and bachelor. The second son, Dread, drove sports cars and was a big-game hunter. The third prince was named Egress (the Wild), a bad drunk, melancholy, a favorite of those fallen from grace of any kind. He was rumored to be dying of consumption. He kept a brace of fighting cocks and a kennel of Staffordshire pit bull terriers and wrote very successful leather-rock song lyrics.

12.

THE STORY IS ABOUT ALL THESE PEOPLE, THEN: THE queen, of course, and the king, the youth in the slick green suit, Orgone, Dread, young Egress, and the loon. The queen's name was Naomi Ruth, the king's name was Egress (the Hearty, sometimes the Bluff). The youth in the slick green suit had many names, all, as it will later turn out, aliases. And the loon was called Loon, sometimes Lone, Lon, Lonnie, l'Ange, Lawn, Lune.

Chapter 2

1.

*N*AOMI RUTH LANQUISHED ALONE AMONG THE GIN-AND-
tonics afternoon after afternoon. Oh, she knew she was
a card, but who was there to enjoy it? Besides, she
never hit her stride till after three P.M. and her fourth
gin-and-tonic, and by then everyone else was at court.
Except, of course, for the servants, whose rapt attention
had thankfully been guaranteed by their station.

2.

SHE TOLD THE SLENDER, HARD-MUSCLED WINE STEWARD
everything she could recall of her childhood—gazebos,
cupolas, domesticated animals with names like Donkey,
Fru-fru, Fluff, and Jingle, her friendly father's ruddy
face as he swung her over his white-haloed head, brush-

ing her back against the cloudless sky, meadows strewn with dipping daisies, golden twilights, lemonade, Mamma, Dilsey, Bubber. . . .

—Jesus, Your Majesty, you're a card! the steward laughed, wiping away tears. —I mean it, he said, suddenly serious.

—Do you? Do you *really?* she queried intently.—I mean, do you *really* think that?

—Yeah. You're a right-on queen. Want another drink?

—Why the hell not? she answered throatily. —Pour.

3.

SPRAWLED NAKED ACROSS THE WINE STEWARD, HER white body splayed like a fallen birch, she asked him, in a detached, impersonal way, as if she were asking herself —What if you were afraid that your husband was gay? Assuming you had a husband, of course. What would you *do?* What would you *feel?* she asked herself.

—Well, the steward answered. —You just never know about these things. I mean, I once knew this rabbi who surprised everyone by going into his father's business. A coat manufacturer. It's like that.

4.

THE WINE STEWARD, LIGHTING BOTH THEIR CIGARETTES with a single match, to Naomi Ruth, the two of them lying on their backs on the llama skins that covered the floor, —Lots of men switch careers in mid-career, as it were. A lot depends on the man's P-factor, the amount of pain he can endure, if you know what I mean. The important thing is that he discuss it with his family and loved ones, even though his decision ultimately may be autocratic. I mean, in the end, it's how you present these things that counts. I say this, Your Highness, because I know you are capable of great forgiveness. For instance, I once knew a priest who became a psychiatrist. Turned out he was happy as a priest, when a priest, and he was happy as a psychiatrist, too, when a psychiatrist, if you know what I mean. So you really never know. Take me, for instance. I may be nothing but a wine steward now, and I'm happy being one, believe me, but I know, if my P-factor is high enough, that I could be happy as, for instance, court chamberlain, say. That doesn't mean I'm not happy as a wine steward, however. No, ma'am, not at all. That's the important part of my notion, but the other part's important, too, of course. . . .

5.

NAOMI RUTH WASN'T VERY INTERESTED IN THE WINE steward's observations. She was interested in his sexual organ. —What do you think is the meaning of life? she demanded.

He shrugged helplessly, as if to say, What can a poor wine steward know?

The queen wept bitter, angry tears. She pounded the pillows with her tiny fists.

He kept shrugging helplessly, trying to look stupid. What a drag, he thought. A fucking drag.

6.

FINALLY, THE QUEEN GOT THE WINE STEWARD'S RATHER large and fortunately erect cock loosened and into her, and she rode him like a log, whooping and slapping him loudly on his hairy, white thighs. For most of the afternoon, they bumped and shoved each other wildly about the room, knocking over furniture, tipping bottles of liquor and perfume, spilling the contents onto the thickly carpeted floor, and sliding with slick rumps across magazines, satin sheets, candy boxes shaped like hearts, velvet-covered love-seats, taffeta gowns, crinolines, silk underwear, a closet floor cobbled with dancing slippers, Turkish towels, talcum, facial greases, squirts of urine, bits of feces, scents, daubs and smears until, eventually, she passed out and he, exhausted and fearful, slipped out and quickly away to the servants' quarters.

7.

NAOMI RUTH FELT NO GUILT. ANGER. ONLY ANGER.
Mainly at the king, but also at the Loon, whoever that
one was. Some kind of freak, she thought. Some kind of
sicko freak. Her heart aching with loathing and revulsion, she broke her thumbs with a small instrument of
torture.

—*Ai-yee!* she cried.

8.

WHAT THE HELL'S GOING ON DOWN THERE? SHE WON-
dered, meaning the court.

—Today's the big day! the king had informed her that
morning at breakfast.

Sensing a significance in the remark, she put her cof-
fee cup onto the saucer noisily and said, —Big day for
what? What's going on? Why am I being left out of
things all the time? I never find out about anything until
after it's happened or been decided. What's going on
today? What's the occasion? Who's coming? Why don't
you tell me what happens down there before it has
already happened? Do you think I'm stupid or something? A child? Do you think that all I can do is ask
questions? Is that why you leave me out of the only life
around here that's worth living? Is it? Is it? she asked.

He looked up from his newspaper and grinned. —What
was the question? he asked.

—*Bastid!* she hissed to no one in particular. That was
when she asked him whether or not he had ever performed a sex act with a man, or a boy.

9.

—MAYBE I SHOULD TRY WRITING A NOVEL, SHE SUG-
gested. A love story, like *Cinderella* or *The Song of
Solomon*.

10.

IN A COLD ROOM IN THE TOWER ABOVE HER CHAMBERS
she wrote, facing an oval mirror on the wall. Whenever
she stopped writing, she looked up and stared at her
own face and long, white neck and smooth shoulders,
her panther-black hair tumbling down in cascades,
her delicate, plum-shaped breasts, her meticulous, ivory-
skinned hands, the single lily in the vase on her desk,
the gold pen, vellum sheets of paper bound in brocade,
her intelligence, passion, imagination, craft. She wondered what it was going to be like as a famous lady
novelist. Then she would go back to her writing. Scratch,
scratch, scratch.

11.

NAOMI RUTH, LIKE MOST NORMAL PERSONS, SLEPT, AND
when she slept, she had a dream. It's possible, there-

fore, that one would wonder about Naomi Ruth's dream. What can be the dream of a *queen?* one would humbly, especially if one were a man, wonder.

12.

SHE RANG FOR THE WINE STEWARD, AND RANG, AND rang, and rang.

Chapter 3

1.

While making his morning toilet, Egress the Hearty thought aloud (so as to better remember his thought): Reality unperceived is form without content . . . and thus the hedonist becomes metaphysician, the mere student of consciousness becomes epistemologist, whilst the phenomenologist ends divided against himself, a self-willed irrelevance for a state of mind. . . .

His broad face covered with a thin film of sweat, the king lapsed momentarily into a deep and intense silence. Then he finished his toilet, washed his hands carefully, and strolled downstairs to the veranda for breakfast with the queen.

2.

EGRESS THE HEARTY, (SOMETIMES THE BLUFF), DUKE of Sunder: son of Donald the Flailer, son of Jack the Boor, son of Moran the Tick-minded, son of Orgone the Tree, son of Hannigan the Pus-filled, son of Bob the Boy-killer, son of Vlad the Sad, son of Roger the Lodger, son of Sigmund the Camera, son of Sabu the Dwarf, son of Egress the Obvious, son of Dread the Courteous, son of Norman the Shopper, son of Grendel the Theorist, son of Warren the Fist-faced, son of Arthur of the Direct Vision, son of Ray the Innovative, son of Ralph the Meatpacker, son of William the Roadbreaker, son of Harry the Hat . . . and so on. . . . to the beginning, the word.

3.

IN ANY KINGDOM, THE MOST IMPORTANT PERSON IS THE king. Period. Everyone should know that, but if someone does not, it doesn't matter. That's how true it is.

4.

IN A HURRY, THE KING TOOK A SHORTCUT TO THE OF-fice, crossing the great yard to a cut stone walkway that bordered the head-high hedge that surrounded the queen's own knot garden. The hedge had been shaped by gardeners, sculptors, actually, into the form of a mountain range, and as he walked hurriedly along the side of the range, he suddenly stopped, for, from the far side of the mountains, he heard the queen weeping. He listened for a moment, and then he thought: The worst thing about being a king is that you're still a man, goddamnit. And a man has *feelings!*

He thumped himself on his broad and thick chest and walked swiftly on, and quoting to himself a poem by Robert Frost, he sang,—. . . and miles to go before *I* weep, *miles* to go before I weep. . . . O!

5.

AS SOON AS HE REACHED THE CARPETED, AIR-CONDITIONED privacy of his inner office, the king picked up his telephone and, bypassing his secretary, personally put through a call to the Loon.

King: Loon? This is Egress. . . .

Loon: Oh. What do *you* want? *More?*

King: No, no, no! I . . . I was just . . . thinking about you, and . . . just wanted to hear your voice, I guess. That's all. . . .

Loon: Well . . . you've heard it.

King: Yes, I have. So, how are you, Loon? Well, I hope?

Loon: Yes. I'm well.

King: Good, good, good. And . . . so'm I. Well.

Loon: Oh.

King: I know I wasn't going to call you anymore, but . . . as I said, I was thinking about you and just wanted to hear your voice. Actually, I had a very

vivid dream last night, a dream in which you figured
rather prominently . . . and you know how it is. I had
this tremendous urge to hear your voice. . . .

Loon: Okay.

King: Yes. Well, good-bye, Lon. Loon.

6.

WHEN A KING IS ASHAMED OF HIS WEAKNESS, TO WHOM
can he speak of it? Any mention would precipitate a
political crisis. Egress kept silent, except when he could
be hearty. He was, before all else, a good and faithful
ruler, in the Victorian mold. —That's got to be worth
something, he said to no one but himself.

7.

FULL OF MELANCHOLY, HE LEFT HIS OFFICE BY A HIDDEN
door and strolled the parapet adjoining, walking along it
to a watchtower at the far end, which he entered. Se-
creted there, he stood for some time peering into himself
near a window that opened onto the great yard and
quarters below, when he glanced up from himself and
saw a figure he recognized as belonging to the wine
steward, saw it exit somewhat furtively, though stagger-
ing, from the queen's apartment, slip through her knot
garden, cut through the hedge, and limp down the walkway to the servants' quarters, where it ducked into the
door that led to the PX.

The king clapped the palm of his hand against his forehead. —Oh, Jesus! he groaned. —Oh, sweet Jesus, what now? I need an unfaithful wife like I need a wine steward!

8.

THIS STORY IS NOT ABOUT WHAT THE KING WILL TELL the Robin Hood figure, the youth in the slick green suit. It's about what happens while everyone waits for him to show up in court after the three days are up and face *down* that brassy bastard of a green-suited youth. So one needn't worry, one is missing nothing, nothing important; for it's all right here in black and white like a series of svelte bruises laid along a frail lady's lovely arm.

9.

THE KING WAS REMINDED OF HIS FATHER, DONALD THE Flailer, who, for no apparent reasons, had beat his eldest son mercilessly, constantly, while never touching the boy's five brothers, except to caress them affectionately. Once, after a particularly bad beating, Egress, then twelve years old, cried out, —Why, Papa? *Why? Why?*

—What do you think should be done with a man who beats women and children? the then-king demanded.

—He should get to a doctor, Egress blubbered. —He's *sick!*

—*Wrong!* the king screamed, flailing his son about the head and shoulders. —You're going to be *king,* goddamnit, and a king has to know that a man like that must be *killed!* When you know that, I'll stop beating you, he promised his son.

10.

EGRESS THE HEARTY LOVED HIS SONS NO LESS THAN HIS own father had loved his. It was a family tradition. So many things simply cannot be helped.

11.

—I WANT THE WINE STEWARD KILLED IMMEDIATELY, THE king said to the Sergeant of the Guard, who ran to the servants' quarters as fast as he could and fragged the PX with a hand grenade, blowing the wine steward to pieces.

12.

THE KING REASONED WITH HIMSELF THUSLY: THE MEANings of most things lie in our descriptions of them. . . .
Explanations, the good ones, are always reenactments.
. . . The man with the greatest access to reality is the man possessing the most comprehensive mode of perception. . . . And that man will end up not merely wise and useful, but also sated, glutted with meaning. . . .

He picked up the intercom and called to his secretary in the outer office. —Miss Phlegmming, come in here, will you? I have a few thoughts I want you to take down for posterity, for The Library.

—Certainly, Your Majesty, she murmured slavishly.

Chapter 4

1.

THERE WERE THREE SONS, AND AT THIS TIME THE ELDEST of the three was Orgone (the Wrestler). He was the best athlete in the kingdom. Twenty-six years old, his supremecy had been recognized for a decade, and though there were a fair number of athletes whose skills in particular sports or events were greater than his, every athlete nonetheless honored Orgone as foremost among them. This was because no athlete was superior to him in two important areas of bodily endeavor: wrestling and copulation.

2.

FOR INSTANCE, ONCE, THREE YEARS AGO, YOUNG RALPH Bunn foolishly beat Orgone (by two-tenths of a second) in the 100-meter run. Orgone immediately threw a double hammerlock on Ralph and fractured both his arms. Then he took Ralph's wife Pearl for a walk under the grandstands, where he screwed her three quick times in a row, dog-fashion, while the excited fans in the bleachers peered down through the slats and, with a frightening ferocity, cheered.

Ralph, lying at the end of the 100-meter runway, unattended, writhing in pain, was full of praise for Orgone's marvelous running ability. —I jumped the gun! he kept insisting.

3.

BECAUSE OF HIS REPUTATION, ORGONE WAS DESIRED even by women who had only heard of him. Naturally, this added to his reputation. Who is more respected as a copulator than the man desired by women who have never even seen him? One defines respect here, however, as a careful form of envy, which is not true respect. Thus it was that a survey taken four years ago revealed that no fewer than 36,312 young men were traveling about the kingdom saying they were Orgone the Wrestler. Shrewdly, Orgone publicized a claim which he hitherto had made only in private, that he could satisfy anyone, male or female, he fucked, and the number of false Orgones quickly fell off.

4.

ORGONE THOUGHT WELL OF HIS FATHER, THE KING, AND treated him with deference. His younger brothers, men perhaps a shade more complex than he, he treated with derisive tolerance. He loved to snap their naked buttocks with a wet towel. *Crr-r-ack!*—Gettin' much pussy? he demanded.

—Fuck off, they snarled in unison.

—Hah! 'Course you're not gettin' any! Little ol' puds like yours, who'd want to get stuffed with weenies like those, when they could have a goddamn *sequoia!* he roared, thrusting his enormous organ out in front of him, letting the warm waters of the shower splash over it.

5.

LATER, SERIOUS, HE SAID TO DREAD, —I *LIKE* TO WORK out. It's as simple as that. To work myself right out of the world. If I push myself hard enough, to extremities that can be reached only if one is already in superb shape and is physically gifted, the only noise I can hear is that of my breath and blood, I see nothing except through a film, I am aware only of my body—and of that I am totally, almost religiously, aware. The intensity is exquisite. The same thing happens when I'm fucking someone. I become the world. All of it. I probably could accomplish the same thing with yoga, but how would it look for a dauphin to be a yogi? It's more *politique* for me to get off on sports and balling.

6.

—YEAH, DREAD MUMBLED. HE CRACKED OPEN HIS BEL-
gian 10-gauge and peered down the barrels at the twin
circles of light at the end. —That's *one* way to deal with
death. But it seems a bit of an avoidance, wouldn't you
say? I mean, why sublimate the inevitable?

He jammed a wad of oil-soaked cotton into one barrel
and ran it to the end with a long, steel rod, catching it
with his tobacco-stained fingertips.

7.

THE YOUNGEST OF THE THREE, EGRESS, WHO HAD BEEN
feigning sleep, rolled over in his bunk and faced the
others. —It occurs to me, he announced in his usual,
pontifical manner, —that you're both in your own ways
protecting yourselves against the proper and necessary
expressions of yourselves as the typical sons of a typical
king and queen in a typical, middle-sized kingdom.

—And just exactly what "expression" would that be,
Mister Wiseass? Orgone inquired.

—Violence, Egress said, smiling warmly. —Talk about
sublimation, he added. —You two might as well be
alcoholics. Or why not drugs? Sports, sex, death—*hah!*
You guys make me laugh. You two run your egos as if
they were government agencies and you meek bureaucrats, he laughed, pitching a handful of eight-penny finish nails at them.

8.

—HEY, KNOCK IT OFF, EGRESS, OR I'LL POUND THE SHIT out of you! Orgone yelled, ducking the nails. Egress turned back to face the simulated-log wall next to his bunk. Dread continued cleaning his shotgun, as if nothing had happened, and after a few moments, Orgone resumed reading his pornographic magazine, chuckling loudly at the cartoons, trying occasionally, but vainly, to interest his brothers in ogling the photographs of the young women's bodies. —Son of a *bitch!* he would cry. —How'd you like to get into *that!* After a while, unable to share his excitement with them, he lapsed into a leering silence and flipped through the pages with one hand, rubbing his lumpy crotch with the other.

9.

WHEN ORGONE HAD FINISHED LOOKING AT THE MAGAzine, he put it down on the floor beside his Morris chair and said, —Listen, guys, I've been meaning to ask you something. What did you think of that creep in the green suit who was at court yesterday, the one Twit told us about? You two move in funnier circles than I do, so what do you think? Is he some kind of suicidal fairy? I mean, is the guy *political?*

He jumped up and started to crank out deep knee bends, his tight double-knit pants bulging hugely at the calf and thigh as he descended and ascended, one-two-three-*four,* one-two-three-*four!* He was able to finish fifty quick ones before either of his brothers could answer him.

10.

DREAD RESPONDED WITH A CYNICAL, WEARY LAUGH.
Then he said, —Aren't you really worried about how
political the old man is?

Crown Prince Orgone leaped to the carpeted floor and
snapped off a hundred perfect pushups. —One trouble
with being in my kind of perfect condition, he said as he
finished, —you have to work harder and harder just to
get a little exercise. I mean, *look* at me! I'm not even
breathing hard!

11.

—WHAT THE OLD MAN *SHOULD* DO, EGRESS SAID, FACING
the wall, —is turn all three of us over to the guy. Then
the question would be whether he had given us to *him* or
him to *us*. Now that's what you call "political," he said
pointedly. —He won't, though. The old man's not able
to think abstractly, never mind act abstractly, for Christ's
sake, he snorted.

Orgone grabbed his sneakers from the closet and made
for the door. —I'm going down to shoot a few baskets,
maybe run some laps. Is that ballboy on duty today, the
crippled one?

—You mean Twit? Dread asked.

—Yeah, the slimy one.

—You like that humpbacked, slimy stuff, eh? Dread
teased good-naturedly.

—Try dope, Egress mumbled.

—Fuck you guys, Orgone said, slamming the door.

12.

ON HIS WAY TO THE GYMNASIUM, ORGONE PASSED THROUGH his mother's knot garden and, glancing up, saw his father staring down at him from the tower adjacent to his private office. To the left of his father, Orgone saw two black rooks fly into the sun. As he entered the gymnasium, a black cat scurried across his path. He shot, and missed, fourteen easy set-shots in a row, and then, ominously, made the fifteenth. After missing seven more, he gave up and ran a dozen laps on the track with Twit, who, later, in the shower, ejaculated prematurely and burst into tears, running from the room when Orgone began to curse. All the towels in Orgone's locker had large rust-stains on them, and he dropped a bottle of body cologne on the tile floor and cut his left foot on a piece of the broken glass. These were omens, and Orgone knew it.

Chapter 5

1.

*F*EELING; IN AN ODD WAY, HURT BY THE GOINGS-ON AT
the court, wounded somehow, and certainly feeling need-
lessly distracted by it all (for, really, what of it concerned *him?*), Dread decided to pack in his gear and
head for Blue Job, where, in recent weeks, there had
been three cougar-sightings of the same, steel-gray, male
cat.

It would be good to kill that beast, he thought, for he
had not killed anything in almost a month, and he felt
the hunger and the deprivation snarling in his belly like
tangled ropes. Besides, the cougar was a big one. It was
a fast one and it was strong, and a very wise and very
dangerous one, he thought.

2.

HE KNEW THE TOUGH, HIGH COUNTRY AROUND BLUE Job as well as any white man did and better than most Indians. He had hunted up there along the wind-shattered sides of the blue, nose-shaped rock for seven summers, night and day, from his thirteenth year to his twentieth. For the first five summers he had hunted with the guides, Abenakis, most of them, and then he had spent a couple of summers up there alone. For five years now—though he had traveled to, and hunted on, every continent in the world—he had not been back to Blue Job. It was almost as if he had become afraid of the mountain, he thought, lacing up his L. L. Bean hunting boots.

3.

HE TOOK NO MORE GEAR THAN WHAT HE COULD CARRY on his own back: a one-man Greenland mountain tent, his down-filled sleeping bag, one pot, one skillet, a Svea gas stove, his Norm Thompson fold-away flycasting out-fit, one change of clothes, and the Ten Essentials: maps (Geological Survey maps of the Blue Job quadrangle), a compass, a flashlight, sunglasses, emergency rations (raisins, chick peas, and powdered eggs), waterproofed matches, a candle for starting fires in dampness, a US Army blanket, a Swiss Army pocketknife, and a small first aid kit. Also, a skinning knife, which he wore on his belt, one hundred rounds of ammunition, and his trusted Remington 30.06 rifle with the special Howard Hughes scope and sight that he had used to such miraculous advantage in Tanzania. —This one helps you kill the big ones, he had written to Hughes.

4.

EGRESS ROLLED OVER IN HIS BUNK AND WATCHED HIS brother finish packing. —Where you going? he asked idly.

—Goin' to the high country, the far outback, headin' for the deep piny woods, lightin' out for the territory.

—Alone, I suppose.

—Alone, Dread said.

—Coming back soon?

—Cain't say, Dread opined. Seated cross-legged on the floor, shoving his gear into the Kelty, he looked like a young, raw-boned lieutenant in the US Cavalry, a noble fool preparing to leave on a dangerous mission behind enemy lines, a secret mission that he, and no one else, had volunteered for. He had covered his pale, freckled face with lampblack and his long, blond hair with a watch cap.

—Why're you done up like that?

—So no one will see me, Dread told him.

—Right, Egress said.

5.

BY DAWN HE HAD REACHED THE SHADOW OF BLUE JOB. Standing in a clearing, he watched the sun inch heavily over the mountain's knobby profile, and he guessed he was now inside the cougar's territory, about eight miles in a line from the top of the mountain.

He began looking for signs, cougar shit, tracks, or a fresh kill, as he walked headlong toward Blue Job. The sun rose higher, and he began to sweat. He could smell his woolen clothing, and he knew the cougar could, too, and it excited him. He shoved three bullets into his rifle and took off the safety and kept on walking, his head facing the mountain, his eyes darting from side to side and down, searching for signs. This was how the Abenaki had taught him, but he did not remember that, for he'd learned it truly.

6.

SUDDENLY HE KNEW HE WAS BEING WATCHED. TURNING around, slowly, like a sleepy cat, he saw the steel-gray cougar crouched about twenty yards away in a short, shallow crevasse between two high, moss-covered rocks. He and the animal stared at each other for nearly a full minute, when, in a single move, the cougar sprang to the top of one of the large rocks and disappeared into the dense underbrush behind it.

Dread felt a chill wipe his entire body. Next time I'll get closer before I look at him, he decided. Then he sat down on the sun-warmed ground for a moment; his legs felt watery, and he was afraid he would fall.

7.

WALKING ON, HE UNACCOUNTABLY REMEMBERED WATCH-ing an Indian woman have her baby in a pine grove, mingling the blood and afterbirth with the warm, sweet-smelling pine needles on the ground. But then he couldn't remember if he'd actually seen that or had only dreamed it and was remembering a dream. He finally decided that it didn't matter: whichever, he had been mightily impressed.

8.

HE STOPPED FOR LUNCH—TEA AND BEEF JERKY—ON THE side of a large, granite outcropping. This time the cougar walked out of an aspen grove at the far end of the outcropping, and, leaping onto the rock, sat there and waited, watching him while he chewed on the dried beef and sipped his tea. They seemed to be studying each other's eyes. Finally, the cougar turned and loped back into the forest, headed east, toward Blue Job.

Dread started to feel a little crazy. —My god, he thought, —who needs to race automobiles at 160 miles an hour, when you can have *this!* He named the cougar Merlin, after his favorite car, a Merlin Lotus Rue.

9.

As HE GOT TO HIS FEET, MOVING SLIGHTLY OFF-BALANCE and too quickly, he reached for his rifle, which he had leaned against the chunk of rock he had been sitting on, and he knocked the gun off the rock to the grassy ground about ten or twelve feet below, where it fired, sending a bullet into the young man's right ear and out the top of his head, hurling him off the rock into the blackberry brambles on the other side, where he had three quick visions, and died.

10.

Dread's First Vision

A HOT WIND ROARING, A TILT TO THE LANDSCAPE, WHICH is quickly righted, and then he is flying through the air a few feet above the ground, when suddenly the flight ceases, and he seems to hover, bodiless; looking down, he sees gray paws and legs, and he lets his tongue loll, and he pants, and for a second realizes that he is becoming the cougar; and then he forgets this, for he has in fact become the cougar, which immediately pisses on a blackberry bush and commences hunting.

11.

Dread's Second Vision

HIS BATTERED, HURT BODY IS WASHED AND ANOINTED with oils and laid out in a white gown and left on a redwood bier in a dimly lit room heavy with the smell of burning incense; he is conscious, sort of, but is unable to speak or move, until a man enters the room, a man wearing an exotically cut, glistening green suit with flowers, daisies, apple blossoms, black-eyed Susans, in his curly hair; and when the man takes Dread's hand, Dread is able to speak and move, as if by magic; sitting up, he steps lightly from the bier and, his hand still held by the green man, says, —Am I the one? —Yes, is the answer, uttered in a melodic voice full of sweetness and light and delicate caring. —The others? Dread asks. —The others are where they have always been. You were chosen to leave because you alone were thought to be the angelic one, the green man informs him; and together, holding hands, they leave the darkening room for the sun-drenched meadows outside.

12.

THE VISION OF TOO BAD: Dread's Third Vision

THE FIRST TWO VISIONS ARE CATEGORICALLY DENIED.

Chapter 6

1.

MEANWHILE, BACK AT THE PALACE, PRINCE EGRESS, alone in the Bunkhouse, (the name given to the apartment years ago by the press, when the boys' rooms had been redecorated with plastic, simulated-log walls, false fireplaces, electrified kerosene lanterns, stuffed heads of mountain sheep, elk, and bear, and for each prince, his own bunk bed), was "getting in touch with his anger."

He strolled through the five rooms of the apartment, tipping over all the furniture, pitching lamps and wall hangings and draperies onto the floor, smashing every piece of glass he could see—windows, mirrors, dishes, liquor bottles. Then, finally, emptying the contents of the closets and dresser drawers onto the floors, he splashed kerosene from one of the lanterns that had not been converted across the heaps of cloth and flipped lit matches into each room, one after the other, and worked his way toward the hall exit. With the rooms blazing behind him, he ran out, passing the just-arriving bucket brigade in the hallway.

2.

HE RAPPED ON THE DOOR OF HIS MOTHER'S CHAMBER and, without waiting for an answer, walked in. She quickly covered her breasts with a satin sheet; she had been brushing her soft, ebony-colored hair. Smiling easily, she said, —Egress, how nice to see you. Will you wait outside for a second, honey, while I dress?

He coughed, wiping his mouth with a lace cuff, smearing it with sputum and blood. —I want to talk with you about something important, Mother, he announced. He could hear the shouts and cries of the firemen and the volunteer bucket brigade in the distance as they doused the flames in the Bunkhouse.

—What's all that sound and fury? asked Naomi Ruth.

Egress coughed again. —It's coming from the Bunkhouse. I just wrecked the place and set it on fire. Vandalized it, sort of.

—Oh-h-h, Egress, not again! she said in a low voice, pulling him to her, pressing his cheek against her soft, white, plum-shaped breasts.

—I'm sorry, Mamma, he said.

—I know, dear, she replied.

3.

FEELING SUPERFICIALLY REFRESHED, YOUNG EGRESS left his mother's chamber. But the old heaviness swiftly returned.

—Good god! he exclaimed to himself. —Is there no

outrage outrageous enough to lift these dead spirits of
mine? Am I doomed, he soliloquized, to an existence of
dull eeks and melancholic squeals with naught but long
intervals of sodden thought between? Oh, daily, daily
diminishes the possibility for suddenness; hourly shrinks
the spontaneous! The hot squirts and jacks of ecstatic
youth are in manhood mere dribbles, and what ere remains of that rough ecstacy now flatly lies upon the
frozen turf before me. I can but prod and poke the
memories as if they were the drained entrails of a goat!
Would a future could be divined there as sharply as a
past! He kicked the loam of his mother's knot garden
with a booted toe. —Shit! he decided. —Guess I'll snort
some coke and go to London and jam. This crap with
the green man will blow over in a few days anyhow. It
won't amount to shit. Nothing ever does.

4.

HE SMOKED HASH AND SNORTED SOME COKE IN THE LI-
brary and, rubbing a couple of drops of hash oil into
each ear, went up to the east-facing parapet to watch the
landscape darken before him while the sun set behind
him. Pretending he was the sun setting was a favorite
fantasy.

This time, however, just as he was getting off, he
heard a ghost. —Eee-gress! the voice called. It was not
an unpleasant voice. —Eee-gress! He looked all around
him but could see no one. The guards were in the watch-
towers. He was alone on the parapet. —Eee-gress!

Well, he'd had bad trips before and had learned the
hard way to "go with it," so he sat down well out of the

bitterly snapping wind and said, —Okay, I'm listening.
Go ahead. There was a pause; then he said, —I suppose
this has to do with the green man. He's been on my
mind a lot today.

—Righto, said the ghost.

—Before we go on, said Egress, —do you mind telling
me who you are?

—You can call me Bob or Jack, whichever you prefer.
It doesn't matter, because I'm only a messenger. We've
never met before and I rather doubt if we'll ever meet
again.

—Okay, Bob or Jack, shoot, Egress said.

5.

AFTER BOB, OR JACK HAD GIVEN EGRESS THE MESSAGE,
which, he told him, was a "plan" from a "source"
whose identity he "could not reveal," Egress went down
from the parapet, caught a car for the airport, and flew
to London, where it was morning. The sun shone and
birds sang. For the first time in months, young Egress
was elated.

Inside the cab from the airport, he snorted more coke
and went straight to where his friends lived, in an ele-
gant, brick townhouse near Grosvenor Square. They
were all members of a world-famous rock band from
California called The Sons of the Pioneers. In the last
few years their most popular songs had been written by
Egress.

—Hey, man! they all cried when they saw him.
—What's happening? they sang.

—Hey, man! he answered.

—Far out! they exclaimed. Then they all sat down on the floor in the middle of the classically proportioned drawing room designed by Sir Christopher Wren and snorted some coke together.

—Good dope, they agreed.

6.

EGRESS SHOWED THEM THE LYRICS TO THE SONG THAT he wanted The Sons to record and release as a single as soon as possible. He told them it was part of a "plan" he had. Then he hummed the melody. —What do you think? he asked.

—Far out, said Mick. He was the spokesman for the group. The others nodded enthusiastic approval.

Together, they went upstairs to the recording studio and prepared their instruments. Egress stood in a corner and coughed on his sleeve, which by now was covered with a thick crust of dried phlegm and blood.

—Hey, man, you gotta do somethin' about that cough, Mick called to him.

—I guess so, Egress said. —Anybody got a clean shirt I can borrow? he yelled. Then he laughed long and loud, which made The Sons of the Pioneers very nervous.

7.

Ballad of the Green Man

(to the tune of "Battle Hymn of the Republic")

Mine eyes have seen the glory
of the coming of the Lord;
He is trampling out the vintage
where the grapes of wrath are stored;
He hath loos'd the fateful lightning
of His terrible swift sword,
His truth is marching on.

I have seen Him in the watchfires
of a hundred circling camps;
They have builded Him an altar
in the ev'ning dews and damps;
I can read His righteous sentence
by the dim and flaring lamps,
His day is marching on.

I have read a fiery gospel
writ in burnish'd rows of steel;
'As ye deal with my contemners,
so with you My grace shall deal';
Let the Hero, born of woman,
crush the serpent with his heel,
since God is marching on.

Chorus:

Glory, glory Hallelujah!
Glory, glory Hallelujah!
Glory, glory Hallelujah!
His truth is marching on.

8.

THE GROUP SANG AND PERFORMED THE SONG WELL, BUT the experience left them shaken, Egress included. It was an aggressively antisocial song, and they knew it.

One by one, they put down their instruments and drifted down the stairs and left the house. As Egress went out the door to the crowded street, he called back to Mick, —Be sure the record gets distributed worldwide by nightfall. I'll take care of any extra expenses.

—Righto, man! Mick replied. Then, to the drummer, Hadley, —Oh, wow, man, that cat is into some heavy shit. Can you dig it? he said.

—Good dope? Hadley asked.

9.

EGRESS IMMEDIATELY CAUGHT A CAB FOR THE AIRPORT and flew home, where it was morning. As he entered the courtyard, he noticed ahead of him a group of Indians in breechcloths, moccasins, and war paint. They carried their Stone Age weapons. He could tell from their facial tattoos and scars that they were Abenakis, "Friendlies."

—What's up? Why the war paint? Egress asked one of the savages, a rotund man whom, because of his slightly arrogant manner, Egress took to be the leader. The others seemed slightly intimidated by the palace and all, which was natural, considering what the wretches were used to.

—We just got paid for cutting trees for the lumber barons, so we kind of decided to drift into town to spend all our money in a few hours of hysteria, the red man said. —Know of any bars that'll serve injuns? he asked.

—There's always the Tam, Egress said. —They'll serve *anyone* at the Tam.

—What we really want is white wimmen, the Indian added.

—Oh, Egress said. —Mind if I tag along?

—Not at all, please do, said the Indian.

10.

ONE THING ABOUT INDIANS ATTRACTED EGRESS MORE than any other: They were in touch with their anger. He used to talk about his attraction with his analyst. —They're so damned self-*entitled!* he would exclaim. —You can take everything away from them, their land, their history, their whole culture, for god's sake, and they still come back at you with that wonderful drunken Indian thing! It's incredible!

And sure enough, when they got to the Tam, all the Indians started ordering double boilermakers three at a time, and in fifteen minutes they were fighting with each other and anyone else who'd hung around. They broke all the furniture and glass in the place and, with Egress joining in, paid for the damage and moved on to the next place, a hotel bar called Lulu's, where, Egress had assured them, there would be "plenty white wimmen."

It was at Lulu's that Egress told the head Indian, whose name was Horse, about the plan he had received from the ghost on the parapet. Horse thought it ridiculous. —You white-eyes really go for that apocalyptic crap, don't you?

11.

—I'LL TELL YOU THE ONE THING YOU WHITE-EYES CAN'T seem to learn from us, no matter how well-intentioned, disciplined, and sensitive you are. It's the distinction between the impulse to anger and the impulse to destroy. Too bad. Some of you make pretty good drunks, and except for that destruction impulse, your suicides are downright attractive, Horse said.

Egress unfortunately didn't hear him. He was eating his glass, and all he could hear was the snap and crunch of a mouthful of shards.

—For example, Horse went on, —an Indian would never break his glass with his mouth, because, for an Indian, the impulse would never be to destroy, not the glass and certainly not his mouth. Rather, the impulse would be to hurl the glass, to create a missile, and if, as a result, the glass were shattered, it would not matter, for it would already have been converted, by anger, into something else. To illustrate his point, Horse threw his own glass into the mirror over the bar and created a beautiful silver explosion. —Intentionality is everything, he said. —Everything.

12.

EGRESS FELL OFF HIS CHAIR, GAGGING AND CHOKING ON his own blood. He had coughed unexpectedly and had torn open his throat with a sliver of glass, and in a short time he had strangled. The white people in the room were horrified and, looking for officials, ran out of the bar into the streets. The Indians knew it was an accident, so they continued to drink and brawl. They only got to town once a month and they wanted to make the most of it. They had liked young Egress, though, and, to honor that fact, they played "The Ballad of the Green Man" on the jukebox over and over, all night long, until dawn, when Horse hallucinated and thought the jukebox was a bear and attacked it with his hatchet. He made a beautiful robe of the skin and wore it proudly for the rest of his days.

Chapter 7

1.

THE GREEN MAN WAS NOT THE REAL NAME OF THE Youth in the Green Suit. Prince Egress had first called him that, rather publicly, and consequently most people took it to be his real name. But, as one may recall, the truth is that he had many names, none of them legal. He was, in all respects, an *alias,* a true underground man. It's not even clear that he was a *man;* he may have been a woman, as well. Thus he was the definitive guerrilla, a person with absolutely no past.

All this, but nothing more than this, was known to the king within hours of the youth's arrival in court and his presentation there of his odd request, or, as some said, his demand. The king, after the youth had spoken, had leaned over to his chief of intelligence, the well-known Grand Inquisitor, and had said to him, —I want that kid's past on my desk this afternoon!

But all he got was an empty manila envelope.

—All right, the king had said, after his rage had fled, —then watch him. The bastard's got to have a *present!*

2.

THE YOUTH IS EXTREMELY ATTRACTIVE, TO MEN AS TO women, although it's not exactly sexual. They stare at him unabashedly wherever he goes. Of medium height and build, he moves with extraordinary grace and purposefulness and seems thus to be both a taller and a stronger person than he probably is. His "costume," upon close examination, turns out to be hand-tailored, somewhat conservatively designed, of a lightweight, finely woven fabric imported either from the Middle East or North Africa, possibly from Greece. The youth himself, however, is a Nordic type. The color of his suit is forest green and is not "slick" or "shiny," as was thought, a mere illusion caused by the way in which the finely woven cloth reflects light. The general impression given to strangers by the youth is that of a person with immense, unquestioned authority. It is not yet clear, however, what exactly his authority is over, for he seems to disdain exerting it.

3.

AFTER COMPLETING HIS ADDRESS TO THE KING, IMMEDiately the youth, hereinafter referred to as the Subject, departs from the court. The crowd eagerly backs off to make way for him. Outside, in the great yard, he is seen talking with Genghis, the Royal Dwarf. A fragment of their conversation luckily is overheard and taken down:

Subject: You're treated *kindly?*

Genghis: Ya, except for all da time ven dey are laffink at me.

Subject: They think you are *funny,* then?

Genghis: Ya! Dey like da vey I am so short in da body und so big in da head. I tink it's kinda fonny myself!

Subject: It must be painful for you, to be treated as other than human.

Genghis: It's a job. I got a family.

Subject: Personally, I think you're disgusting. You should try telling jokes. Make them laugh at your jokes.

At this point, the Subject departs from the dwarf, heading downtown.

4.

AT A BUSY, DOWNTOWN INTERSECTION, THE SUBJECT seems bewildered, as if he is not familiar with the plan of the city. He notices an adolescent girl standing near him, waiting for the light to change. She is wearing a short red skirt, a football player's sweater many sizes too large for her with a huge, red A sewn onto the front, and saddleshoes. She is a schoolgirl.

—Can you tell me where the gymnasium is located? the Subject asks her.

—Hi! she replies. —I'm 37-24-37! Terrific, huh?

—I'm trying to locate the gymnasium. I want to see the famous Prince Orgone run and jump and throw.

—Jeepers, my daddy says I've got the body of Raquel Welch, the personality of Marie Wilson, and the brains of a quail! I *love* the Prince! I've got all his records! Do you *know* the Prince? Jessum, how em-barrassing! I'm 34-27-34! I mean, 37-24-37! How em-barrassing! I can't even remember my own name!

—Are you all right? he asks.

—I'm dying! she cries, and noticing the light has turned green, she scampers across the street, scattering books and papers behind her as she runs. The Subject speaks to no one else and succeeds in getting to the gymnasium on his own.

5.

THE SUBJECT WEARS HIS HAIR IN CURRENT FASHION. HE has little or no facial hair and no distinguishing facial marks, scars, moles, warts, or tattoos. He is quite harmless-looking. Except for his obvious intensity and the fact that none of his graces appear to have been learned (the final grace), he looks like a young man or woman in the diplomatic service. Thus, even though he does not present the proper identification papers, he is waved into the gymnasium area by the guard, is issued a "Distinguished Visitor" pass, and is given the run of the place.

It should be noted that everywhere he goes, the Subject inadvertently reveals flaws, oversights, and malfunctions in the various systems. It is not clear whether this is intentional. If not, he might be of immense use to the systems.

Conclusion: The Subject warrants further study.

6.

HE LEANS AGAINST THE CHAIN LINK FENCE THAT ENCLOSES the playground behind the gymnasium proper and watches the Crown Prince run, jump, and throw. When the prince has completed his exercises and has gone into the showers, the Subject departs, and, as he departs, he drops, or perhaps throws, to the ground the small piece of paper on which he earlier was observed writing:

> *Right-handed, favors left knee and hip slightly (chondromalacia, probably). Will doubtless move to his right when threatened. Large muscles are over-developed, small ones underdeveloped: not as much endurance as he probably thinks he can rely on if threatened. Could be dangerous, if threatened, especially because of martial skills, but can be overcome by almost any opponent using disciplined, intelligent force.*

On the strength of this note, the Subject is arrested and imprisoned, where he presently languishes unafraid.

7.

First Interrogation

Inquisitor: Are you working alone?
Subject: Alone?
Inquisitor: Do you have co-conspirators?
Subject: No. Of course not.

Inquisitor: Then you *are* working alone!
Subject: Well, yes.

Summation: Subject insists no one else involved in his assassination plot.

8.

Second Interrogation

Inquisitor: Did you realize, when you hatched your insidious plot, that in this country assassination is a capital offense? Did you know that we execute assassins?
Subject: I surmised it.
Inquisitor: Aha!

Summation: Subject is not insane, as was formerly thought, and must be judged responsible for his actions.

9.

Third Interrogation

Inquisitor: What is your real name? Your *legal* name.
Subject: Steve Katz.
Inquisitor: Don't fuck with me, wiseass, or I'll break your fingers. What's your real name? We have ways. . . .
Subject: Ronald Sukenick.

Inquisitor: Cut the funny stuff. This is serious! You are in no position to be funny.

Subject: Artemas Ward. Laurence Sterne. Lamar Sabacthani.

Inquisitor: One last time, before we break all your limbs. What's your real name?

Subject: John Doe.

Summation: Subject is hereinafter to be referred to as John Doe.

10.

Fourth Interrogation

Inquisitor: Why were you in the vicinity of Blue Job mountain when Prince Dread was shot and killed?

John Doe: I went there to watch him hunt a cougar. I wanted to know if he was the hunter he thought he was.

Inquisitor: And was he?

John Doe: No. Obviously not.

Summation: John Doe freely admits to having tracked down the Prince Dread on the ill-fated "Blue Job Cougar Hunt."

11.

Fifth Interrogation

Inquisitor: What were you doing at Lulu's the night Prince Egress was killed by the Indian band?

John Doe: I wanted to see if he was as in touch with his anger as he seemed to think he was.

Inquisitor: And was he? No, never mind. Disregard that last question.

Summation: John Doe freely admits to having goaded the child-like band of Abenaki "Friendlies" into attacking Prince Egress at Lulu's.

12.

Sixth Interrogation

Inquisitor: Do you know a schoolgirl named 37-24-37? She claims that you are her father and that you made obscene sexual overtures toward her.

John Doe: I know her only slightly. But I'm not her father, a man who insults and reviles her and who, therefore, is probably the person who made a pass at her. Thus, she's only half-right. *Someone* made a pass at her. But I would never do such a thing. I'm virtually a stranger to her.

Inquisitor: Do you know the dwarf Genghis? He claims you are responsible for his having been fired from his job.

John Doe: I do know him, and I'm glad he's being treated more fairly, but no, I can't claim responsibility.

Inquisitor: Okay, answer this one correctly and you get all the prizes. How did you kill Prince Orgone?

John Doe (proudly): Blood poisoning. You'll recall that he broke a bottle of body cologne in the shower a few days ago and stepped on a piece of the broken glass, cutting his left foot slightly. He should have stayed away from those public showers until after the cut had healed, but he knew he'd go crazy if he skipped a workout. He was trapped by himself, like the others.

Inquisitor: Well said, Mr. Doe. But just for the hell of it, why these three young princes, each in the prime of his life? Why these young fellows? Why not the king?

John Doe: I've got a thing about princes, I guess.

Summation: We've got our man. We've got his plot.

Chapter 8

1.

THE LOON, BECAUSE OF HIS JOB AS JANITOR, OR CUSTO-
dian, for the Star Chamber, a position obtained for him
by the king, had no difficulty in keeping abreast of
developments. He knew more about what was going on
than did the king himself. Unlike the king, however, he
didn't care about what was going on, which is why the
king had appointed him to this somewhat delicate post in
the first place. The king had many faults, but he knew
how to maintain security. He knew that every morning,
after a night of cleaning up the inquisition rooms, the
Loon would go home to his tree house in Central Park
and forget practically everything he had seen, heard, or
smelled. The Loon was much too self-absorbed to be a
busybody.

2.

THE LOON WAS LIKE A BAT. HE SLEPT ALL DAY LONG, from sunrise to sunset, regardless of where he was or what was expected of him. He would, as the sun rose, simply fold whatever piece of cloth there was at hand, a drapery, a rug, a coat, around him like a shroud and drop off to sleep, usually positioning himself in a foetal heap in a corner. The only thing that could wake him was the sunset. In many ways, the habit was inconvenient and sometimes embarrassing to others, but it was a habit he had formed early in childhood and thus he was devoted to it. Actually, all his habits were formed early in childhood, and he was devoted to all his habits. He had not formed a new habit or broken an old one since his fourth birthday.

3.

PEOPLE IN POSITIONS OF POWER SEEMED TO FALL IN LOVE with the Loon, through no design or effort of the Loon himself. There were the director of the nursery school he had attended, the cop on the block, the mayor of the small town in the South where he had spent his middle childhood, the president of the University of Virginia where he had matriculated, the governor of a large industrial state in the northeast, the head of a television network, a Latin-American dictator, a Greek shipping magnate, a US Secretary of the Interior, and, most recently, Egress the Hearty, a king. Only coincidentally were all these powerful persons men, but as a result of that coincidence, most people thought the Loon was a homosexual. They did not, of course, think it of his lovers.

4.

OFTEN, ON LATE-NIGHT TV TALK SHOWS, HE WAS ASKED by the host to talk about whether or not he was, as the host put it, a "homosexual." —Are you, Mr. Loon, a "homosexual"?

—Way-yell, Dick, the Loon would drawl (he had a pronounced southern accent, especially on TV), —since you put it "that way," ah, not *really*.

The audience and Dick the host would roar with laughter, winking and elbowing each other fiercely.

5.

WHEN THE LOON LEARNED, ONE BY ONE, OF THE DEATHS of the three princes, he was surprised but not particularly saddened. He had never thought of them as high-quality persons. All three of them had, at one time or another, jerked off on him while he was waiting, naked, in the anteroom for the king. They hated him, and even if they didn't know it, he did. It was their ignorance, more than the semen on his hairless chest, that had bothered him. The king, on the other hand, had always known he hated the Loon, and thus he never once had jerked off on him. He simply would come into the anteroom and go right to work, buggering the Loon once or twice, and then lie back and tell him his troubles all night long. You had to respect the king.

6.

BECAUSE OF HIS SLEEPING HABITS, THE LOON ATE BREAKfast at night and dinner in the morning. He usually took a light lunch around midnight. Although, as mentioned, he lived in an excellent and completely outfitted treehouse, designed by Michael Graves, he rarely ate at home. Rich and exciting people were always calling him up and inviting him over for breakfast or dinner. Eggs Benedict at nine in the evening with the Loon was regarded as a social event of no mean proportions. This was partially because of the Loon's physical attractiveness (resembling, however, a young Marcel Marceau, he clearly was not "handsome"), partially because of his well-known proximity to power, and partially because of the brilliance of his conversation: He disagreed with everything everyone said, but only by pretending purposefully to misunderstand what was said. He was therefore regarded as an accomplished and dangerous wit.

7.

THE KING LEARNED OF DREAD'S DEATH AT THREE IN THE
morning, when a group of Abenakis, led by the one
called Horse, came in with the body. At four-thirty, he
called the Loon, who had just got home from work.
—Oh, Loon! The queen is mad with grief! She blames
me! he cried.

—Why not? the Loon asked. —You're supposed to be
in charge of everything, aren't you?

—This is no time to be funny, the king said sadly.
—She's blaming me because I'm the one who taught him
to use a gun.

—Oh, said the Loon. —I see. And you didn't teach
him very well.

—Oh, I taught him well, all right, groaned the king.

—No, you didn't, the Loon said sympathetically. —You
can't take all the blame for this onto yourself, Egress.
You taught the boy as badly as you could.

—Oh, no, I didn't.

—Yes, you did.

—No, Loon, I didn't.

—Sure you did.

—I did?

—Of course.

—Thanks, Lone, you've been a sweetheart. I wish I
could talk to my wife this way.

8.

BASICALLY, THE LOON WAS A GENTLE SOUL AND TRIED always to hurt no one. But to avoid exploitation, to keep from becoming "passive," as they say, he was forced to develop certain stratagems. He developed these early in childhood, and because they worked, kept them into adulthood. As can no doubt be observed, one thing he was very good at was "Changing the Subject." He was also good at "Non Sequitur" and "Petitio Principii." If none of these worked and it looked like he was going to be forced into a choice between hurting someone and being exploited by him, he still had two, somewhat extreme, stratagems left: "Fawning," and, if that failed, "Total Surrender." Social scientists have called this last stratagem "Self-objectification," turning one's self into something else, in Loon's case, the exploiter's self. This didn't matter to the Loon, however, because, for him, it was a question of survival.

9.

THAT AFTERNOON, THE KING LEARNED OF THE BARBARous death of Prince Egress. He first called the Loon at four, but wasn't able to rouse him until six-fifteen, when the sun's setting set off a gong inside the Loon's head. Still drowsy, he answered the phone. —H'lo?

—Oh, Lone, Lone! They've killed my baby! Egress, the wild and woolly one, gone, gone, gone! cried the king.

—Who did it? the Loon asked.

—I did it, l'Ange! *I'm* the guilty one! the king hissed into the receiver. —Ask my wife, he added. —She'll tell you.

—Have you asked her?

—No! God, no! These deaths of our children have riven us as a wedge splits a fallen tree. Just when we were really getting it together, too, he said wistfully. —Comfort me, Loon! the king commanded. —Comfort me! My wife doesn't understand me!

—I once knew a man in Oregon who hadn't any teeth, not a tooth in his head. Yet that man could play on the bass drum better than any man I ever met, the Loon said soothingly.

—Do you think so? the king asked.

—Of course.

—You know, I should have connected this to that kinky green-suited guy in the first place! You're a genius, Loon! I'll have him arrested immediately!

10.

—H'LO, EGRESS. THE LOON KNEW WHO WAS CALLING even before he had picked up the phone. He was getting ready to go to bed and was sleepy and cross.

—Oh, Loon, my Lawn, my angel! Doom, doom, doom! the king bellowed.

—He got Orgone, eh?

—Yes, Orgone, my pride, my joy, my crown prince, my dauphin! *Dead!*

—And it's your fault, I imagine.

—Yes, yes, yes. My fault, the king cried excitedly.

—Comfort me, Loon! I need you to comfort me. I need you.

—You *need* me? the Loon asked, incredulous, and wary, too.

—Oh, yes, yes, yes. I used to think of you as my weakness, but now that it's clear to me how much I am hated by my wife, I think of you as my strength.

—That doesn't follow, the Loon said.

—No matter, it's *true!* asserted the king.

—Okay, then. It's not your fault because you did everything you could, the Loon reasoned.

—Yes, you're right, you're right. I did everything I could, the king said.

—Listen, Egress, it's early, so I've got to get some sleep.

—Of course, of course. I'm sorry, I forgot.

—G'bye.

—'Bye. And, Loon, kiss-kiss.

—Kiss-kiss-kiss, the Loon answered. Then he hung up, and, feeling a bit antic, wrapped himself in a flag and went to sleep in a corner of the bathroom.

11.

—OH, YOUR MAJESTY, YOUR PUISSANCE, I'M DEEPLY flattered by your proposal that I accompany you on your pilgrimage to the Empire State Building, but, really, no one so kingly, so majestic, so all-puissant, so inspiring, so inspired, so chosen, so exalted, so with-it, so hip, so heavy, so together, so tough, so mean, so fancy, so witty, so refined, so sensitive, so enlightened, so manly, so kind, so sunny, so benign, so wise, so benevolent, so flexible, so awesome, so handsome, so clean, so sexy, so potent, so resourceful, so brave, so balanced, so sane, so stable, so innovative, so talented, so considerate, so disciplined, so skilled, so patient, so independent, so deliberative, so wealthy, so restrained, so young . . . needs *me!*

—I don't know, maybe you're right, the king said. Kiss-kiss.

—Kiss-kiss-kiss, the Loon answered, letting out a long sigh of relief. If the king's taking off on a guilt trip, let him travel alone, he thought.

12.

—LOON! I'VE CHANGED MY MIND. I NEED YOU. EITHER you accompany me on my pilgrimage to the Empire State Building or I'll kill you.

—I'm yours! the Loon cried.

Chapter 9

1.

THE KING SHOWED UP AT THE LOON'S TREE HOUSE JUST before dawn, and if the Loon hadn't been expecting him, he probably wouldn't have recognized him. He had shaved off his bushy beard and had cut his hair short, rather clumsily, it appeared, with a knife. He looked a little psychotic. He was dressed in a burlap grain bag with holes cut in it for his head and arms and a length of half-inch rope tied around his waist for a belt. He was barefoot. In a small bundle, he had a wooden begging bowl, a string hammock, and a brick-sized bar of solid gold which he said was his Atonement Gift. Evidently, he intended to present it at the Empire State Building.

—Jesus, you're really dressing down for this, aren't you? the Loon observed. —Is it okay if I wear something a bit fancier?

—Whatever, was the dour reply, so the Loon put on a powder blue, wet-look jumpsuit with a long gold scarf tied at the throat.

2.

IT WAS ALREADY EVIDENT, FROM THE KING'S APPEAR-
ance, that the journey was going to be arduous. —Maybe
I'd better bring my credit cards, the Loon suggested
hopefully.

—Whatever, the king replied.

After taking a quick peek into the king's bundle, the
Loon packed one for himself—begging bowl, string hammock, offering (a thumb-sized block of Moroccan hash),
plus a few extras: the Ten Essentials (see p. 44), and his
packet of internationally honored credit cards. —Well,
he announced, —I'm ready.

The king murmured, —Whatever, and they started out
across the park, heading in an easterly direction, toward
Fifth Avenue. They hadn't traveled more than thirty or
forty yards, however, when the sun came up. Immediately, the Loon hung his hammock from two small ma-
ples, wrapped himself in his US Army blanket, and
dropped off to sleep.

The king looked at his companion, shrugged and said,
—Whatever, to himself and sat down on the ground to
meditate. He certainly was a Changed Man, and no one
was more aware of this fact or more impressed by its
significance than he himself, he meditated.

3.

THE FIRST OBSTACLE THEY ENCOUNTERED WAS THE JUN-
gle. It was a dark and moonless night. They could hear
the roars of the hunting beasts and the high-pitched

wails of the hunted. A small, magenta bird with its head torn off fell at their feet. —I think we're in the jungle, the Loon said.

A large, dark jaguar crossed the path a few feet in front of them, dragging with its mouth the broken, bleeding carcass of a spotted fawn, while a pair of hyenas, delirious with barking laughter, followed after. The heavy, moist air was filled with feathers, fur, and the smell of blood. At the river, crocodiles were catching unwary drinkers, peccaries, small deer, armadillos, yanking them into the slow, muddy waters, tearing them apart and devouring them. Snakes fell to the ground with rubbery thumps and rushed slithering after lizards, rodents, small apes, to crush and swallow them.

At last, the sky began to silver at the eastern edge, and they saw a trading post, where they quickly went in and enjoyed a sumptuous Polynesian meal. —Good old American Express! toasted the Loon, raising his rum-filled coconut.

4.

THEY WERE CROSSING THE DESERT. IN THE MOONLIGHT, the sand was like a sea of silver grain. The king, plodding through the sand, silently beat his breast.

—You know, Egress, the Loon said to him, —I was wondering. After you've paid this penance, what then?

—Whatever.

—Jesus Christ! the Loon exclaimed petulantly. —You haven't said anything but "Whatever" since we left! I suppose that's part of the penance, too!

—Whatever, repeated the king, and, in heavy silence, slogged on.

5.

SCALING AND CROSSING THE GREAT SNOWY MOUNTAINS was neither easy nor painless, especially the way they were dressed. At the Divide, they were hit by a blizzard and for three days huddled in a snow-cave, waiting out the storm. They surely would have frozen to death or starved, had they not, on the second day, been joined by a small band of Abenakis. The Indians were fleeing the genocidal persecution of Abenakis that had followed the deaths of Princes Egress, Dread, and Orgone, violent deaths in which the tribe was slightly implicated. Their leader, named Horse, was wearing a jukebox. The others were dressed in the usual flashy, slightly tacky, Indian costumes. They had corn, venison, maple syrup, bread, birch beer, quail, baked potatoes, raisins, apples, and some good New Mexico grass—plenty for all, though the king accepted only a few crusts of bread, which he washed down with snow-melt.

—He's trying to get tight with God, the Loon explained to them.

Ah, the redmen nodded, understanding. They, of course, did not recognize the king, and the Loon wisely thought it best not to tell them.

6.

HORSE AND THE ABENAKIS LED THEM DOWN THE EASTERN slope of the Great Snowy Mountains to the plain, where they parted company. The Indians headed south to New Mexico; the Pilgrims headed north to the Empire State

Building, the prime shrine in the religious life of every
believer in the Empire State. At one time or another
during their lifetimes, most true believers managed to
make it to the great, stone spire, to worship there in
awed silence, perhaps even to join in the traditional
penny-dropping ceremony afterward. The king's all-
consuming passion was the dropping of his gold brick.
He pictured himself standing humbly at the top, head
bowed, dropping his fifty-pound offering over the edge
into the windy, abysmal space below, and at that precise
instant, the very hand of God Himself would reach down
from His perch to touch him on the nape of his neck,
forgiving him, freeing him to return home in a 747 jumbo
jet, King Egress the Hearty, home again, victorious,
self-transcendent, a truly enlightened despot! A grateful
people; a gracious ruler: It would be his finest hour!

7.

ON AND ON THEY WALKED. UNTIL THEY CAME TO THE
SEA, and here they had to stop. The Loon stripped and
ran into the foaming surf, delighted with the chance for a
moonlit swim. He laughed and splashed and called to
the king, but got no response. The king sat down on the
beach and waited. Finally, the Loon came out of the
water, giggling and rubbing his body to warm it. —Terrific
ocean, Egress! You ought to try it. Wash some of that
roadfilm off.

Nothing. What a drag, the Loon thought. If he weren't
such a good walker, I'd think he had tired blood. —Okay,
ol' buddy, he said to the king, —how're we going to get
across? This is your trip, so navigate, please.

Just as the king was about to say —Whatever, a large, silent boat appeared out of the shadows. The boat was of Egyptian design, constructed entirely of papyrus reeds, and was being poled along in the shallow water by a dwarf-like gondolier singing Wagner at the top of his voice. He saw the pilgrims and pushed his sturdy craft in to the beach. —Gif a lift? he queried.

—Do you take credit cards for payment? the Loon asked back.

—Ya, all kinds! Ve got da cross-now-pay-later plans for effrey-buddy! Climb aboard! he sang, and they did, the Loon somewhat apprehensively.

8.

ON THE CROSSING; WHICH TOOK A LITTLE OVER FOURTEEN weeks, the king began to come out of his grim withdrawal. The first break came early the first night out. The dwarf, who seemed an excellent sailor, was whistling aft, busying himself with knots and scrimshaw. The king and the Loon lay on the foredeck, watching the full moon rise out of the ink-dark sea. —This afternoon I dreamed of disaster, the king informed his companion.

—No kidding, the Loon said.

—I saw a bloody moon hanging in a white sky. I saw a museum sculpture garden with all the statues carefully beheaded. I saw four sets of bloody handprints upon a white wall, and every hand was missing the middle finger. I saw two rooks fly into the sun, and only one returned. The king lapsed into a thoughtful silence.

—So what are you going to do? the Loon asked, studying the moon with affection.

—I don't know yet, but I'm beginning to think that my wife had something to do with the deaths of my sons. It's still only a feeling, but a strong one.

—Can you *dig* that moon! the Loon said rapturously.

9.

THE THIRD NIGHT OUT, THE KING WALKED ONTO THE foredeck and saw the Loon lying on his belly, watching the moon rise out of the sea again. The king crept up behind his friend, dropped to his knees, undid the Loon's blue jumpsuit, spread his buttocks, and silently sodomized him.

Finishing, he uncoupled and fell away. He leaned against the mast and began to talk about his childhood, which, to the Loon, sounded awful. The king, however, was speaking with fondness and the kind of hazy nostalgia that often comes over a man on a long sea voyage.

10.

AFTER TEN DAYS AT SEA, THE KING TALKED CONSTANTLY of his wife, the queen, and her nefarious plots against him and his sons. Also, he screwed the Loon at least once a night, much to the erotic delight of the boatman.

—I guess you don't feel so guilt-ridden anymore, eh? the Loon panted.

—Not really, the king said, zipping up the Loon's jumpsuit. —But after all, isn't that what a pilgrimage is *for?*

11.

ONE NIGHT ON THE FOREDECK, THE KING, LEANING EXhausted against the mast, waxed slightly philosophical:—I think that guilt, once perceived, *i. e.,* experienced, is a passion, to be spent, like other passions. The meanings of most things, of passions, certainly, lie wholly in their enactments or in analytical description, *i. e.,* reenactment of those things. The point of human life, when it comes right down to it, is simply to provide content for the otherwise empty forms of reality. The basic difficulty of human life is in knowing when a particular form has been sufficiently filled, or perceived, experienced—knowing when an experience has become redundant. Thus, most of the "good" life is an exercise in good taste, and I do mean ethically.

—Is it safe to assume, then, that you no longer feel guilty? the Loon asked wearily.

—Right! the king said, surprised. —You know, Lon, for a kid with no college degree, you certainly can think abstractly.

—Thanks, said the Loon.

12.

AFTER ONE HUNDRED DAYS AT SEA, THEY DOCKED IN Liverpool, where they caught a train to London, a cab to the airport, and a jumbo jet for home, first-class.

—Good old American Express! the king said, raising his champagne glass in a toast.

—Yay, said the Loon quietly. He was thinking of the block of Moroccan hash he had brought as an offering for the Empire State and how much he was going to enjoy smoking it when he got back to the tree house. —Yay, he said, clinking the king's glass with his own.

—Kiss-kiss, you little devil, said the king happily.

—Kiss-kiss-kiss, answered the Loon.

The king lit a large Cuban cigar. —"Yay," huh? Heh, heh, heh. God, Loon, that's rich! You're such a disgusting faggot, the king said chuckling.

Chapter 10

Remember Me to Camelot

A Novel
By Naomi Ruth Sunder

1.

"*B*E GOOD TO KAY," REX INSTRUCTED HIS ELDEST
son, Bif. "Your mother's never been on her own before,
she doesn't know how to take care of herself, son," he
explained to the boy.

I stood somberly in the center of the living room with
Hunter and Rory, fighting back the tears, proud of our
three little boys, our little men, but proudest of Rex, my
husband, because I understood the deep pain he was
feeling at this, the moment of his departure. He was
leaving us—perhaps forever.

Our country in her need had called him from the side
of his loved ones, and he had no choice but to go. Rex
was a major in the Air Force Reserve, and his unit had
been activated for combat duty in Vietnam, which at
that time I couldn't even have located on a map. They
needed all the veteran pilots they could get, and Rex, in
Korea more than a decade earlier, before Bif was born,
had been one of the best in the skies. He had been
almost legendary, and, as he leaned down to kiss me

5

good-bye, I saw him wink away a tear with a brave grin, and I knew that he was still one of the best.

We kissed, long and joyously, and then he patted each of us on the top of the head and walked out the door to the waiting car.

2.

IT *WAS* TRUE, WHAT REX HAD SAID TO BIF—I HAD NEVER been on my own before, and I didn't know how to take care of myself. I had been the only child of protective parents, raised in Sarasota, Florida, where, as a fifteen-year-old girl trying out for the cheerleading squad, I had met Rex. He was two years older than I, a junior and the captain of the football team.

We fell in love that autumn, the season I made the cheerleading squad and the football team went unde-feated, and from the first, ours was a love that never wavered or wandered off center. Rex was everything I wasn't, and thus it was only with him and through him that I felt completed. He was stern and disciplined, sophisticated yet rough-hewn, gentle but at the same time demandingly straightforward.

And there was a sense in which I completed him, too, for I allowed him to be tender and naive, shy and insecure—character traits he otherwise would have been ashamed of and would have denied himself.

3.

AS SOON AS REX GRADUATED FROM SARASOTA HIGH, WE got married. It was the summer of 1950 and the second half of the twentieth century had just begun. How were we to know that war with the Orientals would break out and, within a year, with me pregnant, would separate us?

Rex went to Texas as an Air Force cadet and earned his wings in record time. I closed up our little apartment, put our wedding gifts and furniture in storage, and went home to live with my mother and father. Three weeks after Rex had left Texas for Korea, I gave birth to our first son, Rex, Jr., whom Rex in his letters instructed me to call "Bif," the name by which he had been known when he played fullback for Sarasota High.

Even from that great a distance, Rex was a doting father. My parents and I would laugh gaily over his long letters filled with careful instructions as to how we should care for his namesake and how my parents should care for me. In some ways, Rex was able to make it seem that he had never left. In my heart, though, I knew how far away he really was.

4.

BUT NOW IT WAS TWELVE YEARS LATER, AND JUST AS the Vietnam War was different from the Korean, Rex's absence from his family was different. Over a decade had passed between the wars, and our life together and our lives separately had changed in many subtle ways.

When Rex had come back from Korea, taller, leaner and, yes, harder than when he had left, we had been able to resume our life almost as if there had been no interruption at all. And in a real way, for, when he had been drafted, our life together had not yet had a chance to begin, there *was* no interruption. As if his absence had never existed, and as if we had not begun at all, we were able to begin anew.

We bought a new, three-bedroom mobile home with a cathedral ceiling in a mobile home park over by the Bay, and Rex went back to work for his father's plumbing company, a journeyman plumber, as before, starting at the bottom, as before. But, "The sky's the limit!" he used to say to me, late at night as we talked in bed of our plans and hopes for the future.

I was newly pregnant with Hunter, and touching my swelling womb, feeling the life stir there, knew how right he was. "Oh, Rex, not even the *sky* can limit *us!*" I would tell him, as he drifted peacefully off to sleep.

5.

HUNTER WAS BORN, A HEALTHY, BRIGHT CHILD, SERIOUS and intense from birth, just as Bif had been boisterous and cheerfully gregarious from birth. Hunter's personality brought out another side of Rex, a side I hadn't seen before. With his second son, Rex was somber, morbid almost, encouraging in the boy, and thus in himself, activities that were solitary, physically strenuous, and somewhat dangerous—such as hunting and deep-sea fishing, rock-climbing, scuba diving. Was this a result of his war experiences, things he wouldn't talk about, couldn't talk about, even to me? I wondered helplessly.

"What else are you going to do with a boy named Hunter?" Rex would tease me whenever I asked him why, for example, he was encouraging his son to hunt alligators in the swamps with Negroes.

"But he's only a *boy*," I would plead.

"A boy's only a small man," he would explain to me.

I was no less concerned over Rex's enthusiasm for Bif's adventures in sports—Little League baseball, Pop Warner football, playing for two or three different teams at a time, day and night, throwing, batting, and kicking balls, sobbing exhausted and disconsolate whenever his team had failed to humiliate the other.

6.

WHEN OUR THIRD SON WAS BORN, I NAMED HIM RORY, after Rex's father, and determined to protect him, if possible, from the several influences of his father that I was fast learning to be frightened of.

As aspects of his whole personality, Rex's fierce competitive pride, his love of sports and danger, and his occasional, dark fascination with solitude did not in any way alarm me. But in our sons, one or another and sometimes several of these aspects became dominant, intimidating, and, eventually, I feared, killing the milder, sweeter traits which, in Rex, made me love him—his tenderness, his shyness, his naiveté, and his insecurity.

Immediately, it seemed, Rex sensed my protective-
ness toward Rory, and he subtly undermined me, encouraging and thereby instilling in his youngest son yet
another negative aspect of his own personality.

"You're like your mother," he would tell him. "All
emotions. Now, your mother is a wonderful woman, and
I'm pleased that *one* of my sons is like her, so don't go
thinking I'm putting you down, son."

But of course poor Rory thought his father was re-
jecting him, so the only emotion he allowed himself to
feel with passion was anger, raging, explosive anger,
even as a child.

7.

THUS IT WAS WITH DEEPLY MIXED EMOTIONS THAT I
watched my husband in his Air Force major's uniform
stride down the steps of our blue mobile home, cross the
pebbled driveway to the white convertible waiting for
him at the curb, pausing a second at the sidewalk to give
Bif's soccer ball a friendly boot into the goal in the side
yard. And then, flinging his flight bag into the back seat,
he jumped into the low-slung car without opening the
door and signaled to the lieutenant to take off, which,
with a great roar of exhausts and squealing of tires, the
lieutenant did.

Little did I know that I would never see my husband,
my beloved Rex, again. If I had known it, or even had
suspected it (I was so enthralled with the man that I
imagined him winning the war quickly and returning
home in a season), I never would have allowed myself to

feel the wave of relief that swept over me as he drove away. I did not then understand that feeling, and naturally I felt terrible for having it, as if I were an *evil* woman. Rex had made my life possible. Without him, I had no reason for living. I knew that I loved him deeply. Why, then, did I feel this hatred for him?

8.

HAPPILY, THE FEELING SWIFTLY WENT AWAY, AND I began to miss Rex awfully. I stayed up late night after night writing long, amorous letters to him (one thing about my Rex, he was a marvelous lover). My days were busier than ever, taken up completely with the boys and my housekeeping.

Then, one night late that summer, I was startled from my letter-writing by a telephone call from the Tampa hospital. There had been a terrible accident, the doctor told me, on the causeway between St. Petersburg and Tampa, and my mother and father, who had driven over to look at a new Golden Age planned community, had been killed. I quickly got my friend Judy from the trailer next door to baby-sit and took a bus to Tampa, as the doctor had suggested, to identify my poor mother and father.

"Yes," I sobbed, "it's they!"

The doctor, a kind, handsome, young man with a blond moustache, comforted me by holding me in his arms. "There, there," he said, "you'll be all right. They went together," he reminded me. "Think how much that would have meant to them."

I wiped away my tears, blew my nose, thanked him for all his trouble, and walked slowly out of the hospital into the cool, palmy night, terrified.

9.

NOW I WAS TRULY ON MY OWN—IN SPITE OF WHAT REX had said to Bif. He had known as well as I that a twelve-year-old boy can't take care of a twenty-eight-year-old woman. He had said it mainly for Bif's benefit, not mine—so the boy would feel the proper responsibility, regardless of whether or not he could act on it.

At first, I had felt sorry for Bif, who was trying hard to live up to the terms of his charge, but then, as increasingly he began to order me around, I began to feel anger toward him. As long as my mother and father were still alive, I was able to get Bif to stop worrying over me simply by assuring him that Grandpa was taking care of us all while Daddy was away in Vietnam. But after the accident, even that assurance was no longer possible.

Then, finally, one evening about six months after my parents' death, all my anger flooded over. I served the boys a supper of turkey hash on toast, leftovers from the roast turkey of the night before, and Bif slammed his little fists down on the table and said loudly, "We never had to eat this crap when *Dad* was at home! What makes you think it's any different now?"

I slapped him across the mouth with my open hand as hard as I could, sending him spinning off his chair to the floor. After calling Judy over to baby-sit, I stomped out and caught the bus to Tampa.

10.

I ARRIVED HOME AGAIN JUST BEFORE DAWN (THE DOC-
tor, Ben, insisted on driving me in his new Buick sedan),
exhausted, slightly woozy from the gin-and-tonics, and
in spite of the endless shame I felt, still raging. The
combination of guilt and anger was almost too much to
bear, and I was afraid I was going mad, though Ben
assured me that I was not, that it was perfectly normal
for the wife of a man away in the service to feel this
way.

I sent Judy home, and while I waited for the boys to
get up for their breakfast, I sat down and tried to write a
letter to Rex. I began the letter many times, tearing each
new attempt to shreds just as I got to the place where I
had to tell him I had let Ben make love to me. I couldn't
do it. I just couldn't make that man's life any more
painful than it already was. I remembered his last letter
to me, received the day before.

*Kay, honey, even though I'm 9000 miles away from you
and the boys, my heart and mind are there with you,
believe me. I still feel that I'm the king in that little kingdom. I feel like a government-in-exile or something, waiting for the signal from you, or from somebody, that it's
okay to return. (Hey, I'd better be careful or the military
censors will think I'm talking politics, eh? Ha ha!)*

At last, I heard the boys happily slamming each other
with pillows, and wearily I got up and started setting the
table for breakfast.

11.

That very afternoon, I received the letter from Washington, D. C., the Department of Defense, informing me that Rex's plane had been shot down by the enemy while on a mission over North Vietnam, and he had been taken prisoner. He was now a POW, and, as far as they knew, he was not injured.

In that one brief moment, as I read the letter, I felt my life turn over and go back to zero and start anew, the opposite of drowning. I still loved Rex, of course, but deep inside, I said a prayer of thanks to the North Vietnamese gunners who had shot him down. I would never be able to explain that gratitude to anyone, I was sure, and I probably could not explain it even to myself, but I could not deny to myself that I felt it, no matter how hard I tried. And though I was not especially proud of the feeling, neither was I ashamed of it.

I joined a group of POW wives from central Florida, and for a while went around with them, speaking to groups of men who were said to have influence in Washington in ways that would somehow benefit the POWs. But I could never quite understand how POWs or their wives could benefit from a more aggressive war policy, so I dropped out of the group. I took good care of my sons and our home, saw Ben about once a month, and just sort of cooled my heels for a while.

12.

GRADUALLY, I BECAME USED TO THE IDEA THAT I WAS on my own and, therefore, had no choice but to take care of myself. I enrolled in night school and got my high school diploma with an ease that astounded me. I went on a diet and exercise program and studied yoga at the Sarasota YWCA. I started sending Rory to a reading clinic, because of his disability, and no longer insisted that the boys get their haircuts where their father had always gotten his. I started trying new foods, exotic dishes, and occasionally took in an X-rated movie with Ben. I took driving lessons, got my license and borrowed the money from a bank to buy a Japanese station wagon.

Rex would have forbidden me to do all these things, if he'd been here, and when the war is finally over and he has been repatriated, he will come home again, and I hope we both can sit down and cry for what has been lost. If he can't do that, I will leave him.

THE END

Chapter 11

1.

IT WAS MORNING WHEN THEIR JUMBO JET WAS READY TO descend, and by then Egress and the Loon were both quite drunk. —Boy, oh boy, Loon, I feel like havin' a party! Le's take some speed an' stay up four days 'n' nights in a row! It ain't every day y'get back from a goddamn pilgrimage, y'know! the king cried to his diminutive friend.

—Hoo haw! Hoo haw! Hoo haw! the Loon carefully responded. He knew how wild the king could get when he was drunk.

Champagne glasses in hand, the two staggered out the door of the aircraft and walked unsteadily through the arrival gate. —They ain't no one here t'*meet* us, the king observed, surprised.

—And it's a good thing, too, the way you're dressed, the Loon said, pointing at the king's grain bag, which was spattered with caked mud, champagne, salt spray, dried semen.

—Yeah, I guess you're right, the king agreed, and they walked to the taxi stand, got into a cab, and in-

structed the driver to take them to the palace. —Toot
sweet! the king said flirtatiously.

—Going to see the queen? the driver impertinently
asked. He was a bent-over, long-haired hippie type who
closely resembled a ballboy who'd once worked at the
gymnasium.

—You betcha! Egress said heartily. He loved the fact
that the driver didn't recognize him. —I'm gonna *fuck*
'er, he confided.

—Yeh. You and everybody else, the driver said,
winking.

2.

WHEN THE CAB PULLED UP AT THE PALACE GATE, THE
Loon saw the handwriting on the wall and decided to
seek cover. —Say, Egress, I'm going to split for my
place, okay?

—Yeah, yeah, sure, sure, Egress said, thinking only
of Naomi Ruth and how happy she would be to see him
again.

As soon as he reached his tree house, the Loon made
a few quick phone calls and confirmed his suspicions.
Just as I suspected, he thought. The queen has taken
over. He made one more call, found out when the next
bus left for his small, southern hometown, and packed a
large suitcase with most of his belongings, his simpler,
lightweight clothes, his chambered nautilus, his five
favorite records, three favorite books, four favorite auto-
graphed photographs of movie stars, and his thumb-
sized lump of hash.

The Loon was not a prophet, actually, but with regard

to political matters, he was practically clairvoyant. This was doubtless because he himself was as apolitical as a four-year-old child. With his talent, he ought to have been made the premier political advisor in the state. But, ironically, the very thing that gave rise to his talent disqualified him as a councillor: he had no loyalties whatsoever to anyone, except as he himself was personally threatened or rewarded. His politics were based entirely on what he saw as necessary for his own continued survival. This did not, however, make him amoral, for, in all his personal dealings with people, he remained both generous and kind.

3.

EGRESS THE HEARTY STRODE MANFULLY INTO THE GREAT Hall and roared, —Honey, I'm home!

The tapestry-covered walls soaked up his noise and left him standing alone in silence. —I like the way she's decorated the place, he mused, fingering one of the thick tapestries. —French. Then he saw her, standing on the dais at the far end of the enormous room, and he ran, arms spread wide, to her. —*Baa-a-a-bee-e-e!* he bellowed.

After he had kissed, hugged, and fondled her a while, he began to realize that she had not responded, that she had stood still throughout, as if she were made of alabaster, silent and motionless and cold to the touch. —What's the matter? Aren't you thrilled to see me? he asked her. —Hey, baby, he growled in his sexy voice, —you really turn me on when you hold it back like this. He started to paw her breasts.

But still there was no reaction. —What the fuck . . . ?

he exclaimed, drawing back to look at her. Maybe she had the rag on or something. You never can tell.

Finally, she spoke to him in a low, calm voice. —Egress, you've been gone for more than seven years, and in that time I've acted in your place. . . .

—Fantastic, terrific, he said. —That's why you're the *queen*.

—And in those years, she went on, —I've made a number of decisions, executive decisions. Foremost among these is the decision that I am to remain the chief executive, even after your return. I am, to put it simply and crudely, taking *my* turn, she declared.

—If you were a fucking man, he hissed, —I'd kill you. But you're not. You're a woman. My woman. Now, c'mere and give me some ass.

4.

A TROOP OF ABENAKIS EMERGED FROM BEHIND THE ARRAS next to the queen, and at a signal from their chief, the one called Horse, they surrounded Egress and tied him with deerhide thongs and pitched him onto the floor in a heap at the queen's feet. Egress was beginning to feel a little frightened. —You're *serious!* he exclaimed to her.

Not answering him, she turned and regally left the hall.

—Horse! Don't you recognize me, man? I'm your king! It's *me*, Egress the Hearty, for Christ's sake!

—Yeah, I know who you are, the red man answered. —Or rather, I know who you *think* you are. The fact that you think you're still in charge, though, just because you're who you are, doesn't mean goatshit around here anymore. It's hard to run around claiming Divine Right when you ain't got no Enforcer! Horse joked, leading his band over to one of the far corners of the room. He was still wearing his jukebox, and one of the warriors punched E-5, a Buffy Sainte-Marie tune, and the group formed a small circle and started to dance.

—For god's sake, don't you guys have any loyalty to your own *kind???* the king shrieked at them. —Where are your *balls!!!* Egress was beginning to comprehend what was happening, and his fear had turned to rage. Trussed up like a pig in a market, he roared, thrashing and rolling himself about the room.

Sadly, while the other Indians danced, Horse watched him. —The only good king is probably a dead king, he murmured to himself.

5.

THIS IS HOW EGRESS ESCAPED: THE ABENAKIS, AS RED-men often will, took to drinking, and after having exhausted themselves with brawling, singing, and dancing, fell asleep in a pile in the corner. At dawn, a young girl, coming from one of the barracks rooms where, apparently, she had been visiting her boyfriend or her brother, stole across the Great Hall in the half-light and almost stumbled over the fuming body of Egress.

—Watch it, for Christ's sake! he snapped.

—Oh, golly, I didn't see you there! I'm *terribly* sorry, she said sincerely. She was wearing a high school cheer-leader's uniform and had large, pointed breasts. —Are you all right? she asked the king.

—Listen, I was captured by some Indians working for my wife, the queen, because she hates men. Do *you* hate men, too? he asked kindly.

—Oh-h-h, gosh, *no!* I just *love* them! I mean, I have too much *respect* for men. I'm 37-24-37, you know, she said proudly.

—That right? Well, then, why don't you just untie me, honey, so I can stand up and get a good look at your body?

—Oh, I'm so em-barrassed! she giggled, bending down to untie him, brushing his nose with her naked thigh as she worked.

When she had freed him, he stood up, grabbed her by her left breast, and together they ran from the room to the courtyard outside. There he leaned her against the wall, yanked down her panties, and stuffed his stiff cock into her. He pumped half a dozen times, came, and quickly withdrew, saying as he left, —I'll be in touch.

—Bye, she said weakly.

—Don't forget to douche, he warned her.

6.

EGRESS DECIDED SWIFTLY THAT THE BEST WAY FOR HIM to get his throne back was to go underground, at least until he could size up the situation. He called the Loon, but there was no answer. —The little bastard's probably hiding out in Biloxi, he cursed.

The streets were filled with Indians carrying weapons and wearing makeup on their faces. —Goddamn faggots, he said to himself. —They'll work for anyone who'll let them paint themselves up.

With his back to the street, the door of the phone booth closed, he made one more call, to a number his security chief had given him years ago. —H'lo, he said when the party answered. —Is this the Underground?

—Ya.

—Good. I need to drop out of sight for a while. You know what I mean. Can you arrange it?

—Ya, I tink so. How many iss dere in your party? the man asked.

—One, Egress said.

—Und vat time may ve expect you?

—In about fifteen minutes.

—Ya, dot's fine. Und vat iss da name, pleese?

—Sunder.

—Tank you for callink us, Mister Soonder. Ve vill be expectink you, den.

Hanging up the receiver, Egress darted out of the phone booth and leaped into a cab that had just pulled up to the curb. The driver was a tiny man, so short he could barely see over the steering wheel. —Vere to? he asked.

—Underground, Egress commanded.

—You iss da Soonder party?

—Yeah, that's right.

—You are early, Mister Soonder.

—Yeah, sorry about that. I got away earlier than I expected, he explained as the cab sped away.

7.

THE DRIVE TOOK HIM TO THE CLUBHOUSE OF A LONG-abandoned golf course in one of the suburbs. Inside the shuttered building, a low, ranch-style, log structure covered with vines and moss, a group of men and women, mostly young, long-haired, and filthy, were making bombs and various incendiary devices. They greeted him with silent, agreeable nods and continued with their work.

Egress admired their discipline and decided to tell them who he was. When he had finished speaking and the laughter had died down, one of the group, a slender youth with flowers tangled into his hair, took Egress aside and said to him, —You may not remember me, but we've met. I know who you are, who you *were*, he said in a confidential voice. —These kids, they're rather heavily into revolution, so they're not going to be of much help to you, except to hide you out for awhile—but they'll do that only so long as they think you're a little crazy and are wanted by the State. That grain bag you're wearing helps, also that psychotic-looking hair cut. You look like Richard Speck, he said with a snicker. —But you're going to have to be more careful, he went on. —They're serious about this revolution thing. . . .

—Wait a minute, Egress said, interrupting him. —Aren't you . . . ?

—Yes.

—But I thought I ordered you executed!

—Yes, you did, but your wife countermanded your order and had me freed right after you left on your famous pilgrimage. She thought I was gay, and there was an amnesty offered, and so. . . .

—I thought you were gay, too. Aren't you? the king asked, incredulous.

—Not *really*. But never mind all that. If you want to hide out here, you better start acting crazy, and you better start helping make the bombs. You'll find that your family problems won't count for very much here, not with this group, he chuckled, leading the king back to the young men and women at work on the floor among the wires, fuses, gasoline, and dynamite caps.

8.

LATE THAT NIGHT, WHILE THE OTHERS SLEPT, THE KING rolled over on his pallet and whispered to the Green Man, who was lying on the pallet next to him. —Are there any others left, besides you, who have remained loyal to me?

—A few, I imagine, the Green Man answered, yawning. —And you really can't count on me for much more than company.

—How many are left? the king persisted.

—Ten, maybe.

—*Ten!* Ten men! Ten loyal men. Ten stout-hearted men! he whispered with growing excitement. —Okay, Greenie, you and I are getting out of here now, he announced.

—What for? I like it here. I mean, hiding out isn't a bad way for a man to spend his life.

—Not this man, fella. We're getting out of here, and we're going to contact those ten stout-hearted men and get them together as fast as we can, tonight, if possible. And by tomorrow night, we'll have ten thousand *more!* he almost exclaimed.

Once outside the house, the king asked him, —Which of the ten is closest to where we are now?

The Green Man told him of Twit, who used to work at the gymnasium and now was a student of Oriental religions and a part-time cab driver in the city. —He's kind of wacky, though. Childhood traumas, asthma as a kid, that sort of thing. He's very big on exploring personal power potentials—mysticism, karate, scientology, peyote, Sufi rites, etc. But he's still very loyal to you. I think he's Jewish, he added.

—No matter. He sounds okay to me. Extremism in the defense of liberty means a man like that can be trusted. You'll see. I wasn't king for all those years for nothing, y'know. I'll make him a general. I know the type, he said as the two of them set out in the dark for the city, where Twit maintained a flat.

9.

AFTER TWIT WAS APPOINTED FIRST GENERAL OF THE Loyalist Army, the king, the Green Man, and the new General set up their headquarters in a hidden canyon far in the countryside west of the city. They pitched a high, conical tent and ate free-ranging prairie chickens shot on the wing while they waited for the army to gather, as they knew it would, once word of Egress's return leaked out.

The first volunteers showed up around noon—the world-famous rock band, The Sons of the Pioneers. They came roaring into the canyon on matching, ruby-flecked, Harley Davidson motorcycles. —Hey, man, what's happening? the leader of the band said to the king, and the king quickly explained.

—Far out, the musician said. —You want us to do a fund-raiser or somethin', man? he offered.

Introducing the group to General Twit, Egress agreed that a fund-raiser would be fine, but not till after the war. Meanwhile, he wanted them just to let the fact of their endorsement of his project get around, maybe hold a press conference or two, that sort of thing.

—When this thing hits the media, he said to the Green Man as they strolled out to the dusty plain to hunt prairie chicken, —we'll be in! Every mother's son in the fucking country will be fighting on our side! Let

Naomi Ruth *have* her minorities. *I'll* have the rest. Don't forget, these kids have never had a chance to fight for something they *believe* in! he reminded his cohort.

10.

THAT NIGHT, LYING ON HIS COT IN HIS TENT, THE KING had a dream which confused and troubled him. He dreamed he was the pilot of a fighter-bomber on a bombing mission over North Vietnam. Sweeping down on his target, a Standard Oil refinery operated by the enemy, he released his bombs and then suddenly realized he had overshot his target by about five miles. As he pulled the nose of the plane skyward, he glanced out the canopy to see what in fact he was bombing, and he saw three little boys standing in the middle of a clearing in the jungle. For an instant he saw their faces, recognizing them, and then they were gone. And then he heard the sickening sound of the bombs exploding in the clearing in the jungle. All the way back to the base in Laos, he roared with incoherent pain.

The Green Man, mercifully, woke him, but when he told the king that the army was ready to march on the city, the king began to sob uncontrollably. —No, no, this is *insane!* What are we *doing?* We're *killing* each other!

The Green Man gave him a couple of ten-milligram Librium capsules and got him calmed down again, so that, by sunrise, Egress was once more his hearty, unshakable self.

—I always have a nightmare the night before a big battle, he explained to the Green Man as they rode toward the city at the head of the motorcycle corps.

11.

BEHIND EGRESS, GENERAL TWIT, THE GREEN MAN, AND The Sons of the Pioneers, the Loyalist Army spread out like a gigantic cape all the way to the horizon. Most of the police and military, practically all professional groups, athletes, clergymen of all the more popular faiths, many clerk-typists and petty bureaucrats from the civil service, members of all the building trades unions, motorcycle gangs, automobile mechanics, miners, realistic novelists, coaches, and all the youth of the land who had been about to apprentice themselves to members of these groups (but who were, in actuality, probably attracted to the Loyalist cause by the presence of The Sons of the Pioneers) turned out to have remained loyal to the king. They seemed to have been waiting only for the proper opportunity to express that loyalty. There were, of course, legions of older men who had wanted to join the battle on the side of the king, but, because of their age, had been put to better use as medics, service personnel, councillors, etc. Stationed with them at the rear of the marching army and at the canyon headquarters, the numerous women who had joined the army had been put to good use making uniforms, bullets, tents, and victory banners.

12.

ON THE WAY INTO THE CITY, THERE WERE A FEW ISOLATED skirmishes, quick forays by small search-and-destroy units into farmhouses and crossroads hamlets where the inhabitants had tried to resist the king's army, not so much because they were loyal to his wife, but rather because they were out of touch with the conflict and thus had no loyalties at all. The sheer mass of the Loyalist Army overwhelmed them, and the raping, looting, and slaughter that followed barely delayed the army in its march. Like pebbles in the path of a river that has burst its dam, they were swallowed whole and caused not even a ripple of hesitation. But when the river reached its destination, the city, it crested, then swirled, eddied, slowed, and finally ceased movement altogether, as if, blocked by a second dam, it had emptied into a new, unexpected basin, creating in a short time a huge, motionless lake of bewildered men.

The city was deserted, empty, and all the major buildings had been destroyed. The streets were filled with rubble, concrete, wrecked automobiles, buses, trains, mattresses, broken cases of food, furniture, clothing, and glass, as if there had been an earthquake and it had occurred at the one moment when everyone was out of town. Egress was at first astonished, and then, when he had begun to piece together what had happened, a process in which he was aided by the Green Man, he was deeply depressed. One might say broken.

Chapter 12

1.

(At the Airport)

HE RECOGNIZED HER BY THE NAPE OF HER NECK AND his powerful attraction to it. She stood motionless in front of him, like Leda before the swan or Europa before the bull, waiting her turn to purchase a ticket, presumably for the next flight out. There were no longer any arriving flights; departing flights had been doubled.

Hungrily, he stared at the tendons on her neck, the fine strands of hair lifting like an Elizabethan tune toward the high, severe tail of her haircut. It was in the new style, he noticed, the one called the "French Barricade." She curled her head forward as she drew a credit card from her purse and, handing it to the harried clerk, paid for her ticket. Egress ached to strum the taut muscles of her neck, the braid of tendons and sinews that ran like Greek bread from under her ear lobes to her shoulders. He felt his hands open out, reaching like morning glories at dawn, his fingertips swarming with impatience for heat.

She accepted her ticket from the clerk, turned brusquely and saw him standing there behind her. —Oh! she said, clearly startled. —Surprise, eh?

—Ah . . . yes! Surprise-surprise-surprise-surprise-surprise, he said mockingly, cursing himself for it as he spoke: —Goddamn you, goddamn you, goddamn you . . . , he cursed.

—It's your turn, I believe. The man is waiting, Egress, she reminded him, inclining her head in the direction of the uniformed clerk at the counter. She seemed to have a sarcastic smile on her thin lips, as if she felt superior to her husband.

A short and exceedingly fat woman with a pair of long-legged, unhappy, teenaged sons stood in line as a group behind Egress. She kicked one of her large suitcases along the floor until it crashed into his heel, battering his Achilles tendon with it as she kept on kicking. Her arms, like meat-filled pillows, were folded pugnaciously across her huge breasts, and, while swinging at her suitcase with one stubby foot, she glared intolerantly at Egress and Naomi Ruth.

—*Next!* the clerk pointedly called out.

—They think they're in a movie, the fat woman muttered to her sons.

—Okay, okay, I'm next, Egress said, turning for a second to the clerk, saying to him, —One way, please, and when, a second later, he looked back, Naomi Ruth was gone.

—One way . . . to where, mister? the clerk impatiently asked him.

—Oh. Ah . . . Nevada. Reno, Nevada.

—First-class or tourist?

—Ah, tourist, tourist. Yes . . . tourist. He placed his credit card onto the counter in front of him and the clerk ran it through the machine and handed it, with the ticket, back to him.

Egress deftly stepped away and slipped into the crowd as if slipping into a broad, slow river, and let the current carry him. He said to himself, I've never felt so tired, so bone-weary. I feel a thousand years old. I wish I'd been born a member of a different race, one with more of a future. I almost wish I'd been born a woman.

Oh, but just the same, thinking that one over, he thought, I'm glad I don't have to be born again as *anything*. The risk isn't worth taking, he observed shrewdly. Maybe everything's only as decently worked out as possible. It's hard, to run off and turn your back on the fact of your own manhood, when you are a man and have been one all your life. I mean, what the hell, an ego's an ego, and you sort of have to take it as it comes from where you get it. Right? he humbly asked himself.

Right, he declared with confidence, sliding forthrightly along with the crowd and keeping a sharp lookout for the proper boarding gate and any possibilities of Naomi Ruth.

2.

(On the Beach)

EGRESS SAT ATOP THE SMOOTH, SOW-SIZED BOULDER, looking out to sea, diddling idly with memories of his childhood. The harsh cry of a gull caused him to look to his right, along the gray beach, and though he could see little more of the figure walking toward him than that it was a woman's, he knew immediately that it was Naomi Ruth's. The languorous yet sporty walk, that slow movement of muscles hardened leisurely by tennis, could belong to no other woman, certainly to no other woman in *his* life, which, at that exact moment, he realized, in terms of the number and kinds of women he had studied closely, had been rather oddly narrow. Was that *usual?* he wondered. Was he, then, therefore, lonelier than other men of similar means and abilities? Was this, the catastrophe of his middle age, his *own* fault?

She didn't give any sign of recognition until she had drawn near enough for her to speak to him, when she said simply, —I never thought of you as a sun-worshipper, Egress. She was wearing a tiny, cerise, two-piece bathing suit. He had on a rust-colored tanksuit made of wet-look nylon. They both had good tans, leathery brown and evenly distributed.

—Having a good time? he asked.

—Yes! And you? She sat down lightly beside him on the rock and looked out to sea.

Egress looked out to sea also. —Yes, I guess one *could* call it that.

—What?

—A "good" time.

—Oh.

—I mean, I've been "good" lately. Travel and most other forms of inactivity, as you know, produce in me a certain . . . "morality," he said carefully.

—That's pretty decadent-sounding, Egress, she said, laughing. —You were many things, but I don't remember you as particularly decadent.

—I don't know. No, I don't think I was, not at all. Nowadays, though, well, maybe I am. After all, life has to go on, *n'est-ce pas?* "The old biological imperative," as the Loon used to call it. . . .

—The *Loon!* she sneered.

—Oh, you can't blame *him*, Naomi. Not for this. He was weak, that's all, and he knew it. For him, everything had to come down to that old biological imperative. His one ethic, his only possible morality, was survival, for god's sake. We shouldn't go off projecting our own alternatives onto him, not now. That's just too easy. . . .

—I know, I know. It's just the associations. They're still very strong, you know. And painful.

—Sure, I understand. It's the same for me—though of course I'm termperamentally slightly more existential than you.

—That makes it easier, probably.

—Aw, please, Naomi, I happen to treasure this moment, so please, don't indulge in sarcasm. Not now.

—Sorry.

—As a matter of fact, just as you came walking up, I was sitting here wondering whether or not this whole thing was my fault completely. I mean, *completely*.

—Completely?

—Yeah. Except for a few things, of course. All that destruction at the end, for instance. I mean, Jesus, Naomi, you could have just "left" me, you know. All those innocent people! he exclaimed compassionately.

—Nobody's "innocent," she said grimly. —It's Greek, and that means everything's interlocked. When the House of Atreus finally collapses, the entire city has to collapse around it. *I* had nothing to do with all that destruction at the end, not personally, any more than you did. Not as much as you did, if you ask me, from what I heard. What were you doing when you went underground, anyhow? Working as some kind of secret double agent? No, I'm sorry, I don't mean that. I know you had nothing *personally* to do with all that violence and destruction of property at the end. It was just coincidence. Fate.

Egress sighed with evident relief. —If that's true, then

maybe the whole thing wasn't my fault, not entirely. Right?

—Who cares about "right" now? she asked rhetorically, leaving the rock. —Good-bye, Egress. I'm glad you are having a good time, however decadent. I don't miss you, but I wonder lots of times how you are now.

—Same here, he said. —Are you "lonely"?

—Yes. But as I said, I don't miss you.

—Right. Same here, he said to her lithe back as she walked athletically away.

3.

(In the Museum)

HE HAD STEPPED INTO THE MUSEUM TO GET OUT OF THE rain, a sudden, unexpected shower that probably would not last. I never seem to have an umbrella when I need one, he thought, as he glanced into the adjacent roomful of midnight blue, very abstract paintings. The paintings, recent acquisitions, evidently, were all about six feet square, covered completely with a smooth coat of midnight blue paint. The surface was so smooth that it seemed to have been applied with a large roller or spray gun. There were between twenty-five and thirty of the paintings hanging in the large room, distributed evenly along the walls and hung at exactly the same height. Egress found himself moved invitingly by the sight and went into the room for a closer look at them.

They were by an artist whose name he did not recognize, and they were entitled, "Composition A," "Composition B," and so on, in sequence, all the way, he discovered, to "Composition Z," which brought him back to the door again. The exhibit gave him considerable peace of mind, and it was with pleasure and a kind of relief that he noticed, after having gone through the exhibit a second time to study each individual painting closely, that he was the only person in the room—until the moment when Naomi Ruth, in a lemon yellow dress and carrying a matching yellow umbrella, entered the room.

—Oh, she said, seeing him. —Well, we meet again. We can't go on meeting like this, she laughed, shaking her small, dark head provocatively. —Are you enjoying the paintings? she queried.

—Oh, yes, immensely. As a matter of fact, they have given me a great peace, a deep spiritual equilibrium which lately I seem to have lacked to a considerable degree. They've offered an order to my chaos.

—The artist is my present lover, she said in a flat voice.

—Ah? Ah, well . . . ahem, how shall I say it, then? How nice? Or, perhaps, congratulations? Or would it be more polite to admit a personal relation and hope he's like his paintings—that is, lucid, totally consistent, witty, and well-hung. He smiled coldly at her, pushed past and out the door, broke into a flagrant run and exited from the museum to the downpour outside.

4.

(At the Café)

—ACTUALLY, I'M ALL RIGHT NOW. THINGS ARE MUCH better for me, he assured her.

—*Are* they? Good. I was worried, she said, motioning with one hand for the waiter. The waiter arrived, and Naomi Ruth ordered their drinks, in French, which impressed him, for her accent was quite good.

—Yes, I have a girl friend, a good woman who loves me well, he lied. —We share a nice little flat in a charming quarter of the city. Very comfortable place. A lot of Russian émigrés live in the district. We're very happy. She's a dancer. Quite young. Lovely. Smokes those Russian cigarettes. Young. A sparkling beauty. Tanya. She's Russian. A dancer. Quite young. She loves me.

—Ah, good. And you? Do you love her as well? The waiter brought their drinks, a martini for Naomi Ruth, Campari and soda for Egress.

—Oh, well, you know. As I said, she's quite young. Let's just say that I'm "fond" of her, and grateful. She's a marvelous dancer. Flying feet.

—How nice, said Naomi Ruth, nipping at her martini with pursed lips. Though she didn't believe a word he said, she judged him as she would if she had believed everything. The man's still a cad, she decided. Even his lies betray him. It's no use. —It's no use, she informed him.

—No?

—No, she said, getting up from the table.

—Must you rush off?

—Oh, I left long ago, Egress. If only I could get *you* to leave, I'd be a free woman, she declared, and she picked up her coat and walked hurriedly away.

He finished his drink slowly, thoughtfully, then, brightening, drained hers. He suddenly felt like celebrating.—*Garcon!* he called. —Bring me a double martini, *s'il vous plait!*

5.

(In the Hansom Cab)

—WHERE *MY* MONEY COMES FROM SAID EGRESS TO NAOMI Ruth, is not of much importance, you know that. After all, it doesn't matter to *me* where it comes from, so why should it matter to anyone else? Most of my economic theories are of the type used to describe other people's financial situations, not one's own, which happily places me in the grand tradition of modern economic theorists, and also leaves me free to take whatever I can get from wherever I can get it without offending the glorious abstract—letting the general principles freely transcend the particularities of my usually very complex finances. So, the answer to your question, What am I doing for money these days? is, casually, I get by. What about *you,* however? Since you happen to be a woman and thus have spent most of your life locked by the abstract into a very particularized and personal dependence on other individuals (first your father and then me) for your money—to the degree that your most important personal relations have been, as they must be, with whomever you have economic relations—What are *you* doing for money these days? Asking a woman about her financial life is not much different from asking her whom she's sleeping with, I know, and if you had not slept with me for twenty-five years or more, believe me, I would not feel entitled, as I do, to pry.

—I get by.

—We're quite a pair, Egress laughed, aren't we? It's a damned good thing nobody's counting on us to play big historical roles, to lead his revolution or put one down.

Naomi Ruth responded with a chuckle. Egress, leaning forward in the seat, called to the driver and instructed him to stop at the next corner, in front of the American Express office. Then, to Naomi Ruth, he said, —Well, I'll leave you here. It's been kind of you to share your ride with a walking-man, a member of the walking class, heh-heh. Seriously, though, thanks for the lift. I might've had to stand there for hours before convincing a cab to stop. The hansom cab stopped in front of the American Express office. —Well, here we are! Good old American Express, eh? By the way, if you're going to be here in the city for a few days, maybe we can get together for lunch . . . ?

—No.

—Right, right. Bye, then.

—Bye.

Exit Egress cheerily. Naomi Ruth signaled for the driver to go on. Exit hansom cab.

6.

(At the Plaza)

—AH, YOU BREAKFAST AT THE GREEN TULIP ROOM? I didn't realize. . . .

—Well, yes, I've been coming here on Sundays for several months, all winter, in fact. It's a bit ornate, but

quiet, peaceful, and of course there is the food, and the
service. . . .

—Yes, the Plaza. . . .

—What about you, is this your first time, I mean, for
breakfast?

—No, not really. I mean, not that I haven't dined here
before, as you must remember. . . . We stopped here
many times together, for lunch, remember? Never on
Sundays, though. Oh, will you listen to me, making
jokes like that! It's so difficult, though, when you reach
a certain age, I guess, to avoid references either to the
past or to the popular culture . . . so difficult just to be
personal and immediate. I'm sorry about that.

—You think it's *age*? That we've gotten so old, or so
tired, that now our lives are either in the past or "public" . . .? I wish *I* believed that. I'd give up fighting it, if
I thought it was an impossible fight to win. I'd let myself
go, either into the past or into the public life, you know,
that fantasy of one's life as a movie, or a TV series, or
maybe a *Time* magazine cover story. . . .

—Which appeals to you more?

—I don't know, to be honest about it. Today, seeing
you, here, on an early spring morning, with all this
hushed, tasteful luxury around us, I think I prefer the
past. But any other time, when the associations aren't
so strong and aren't especially pleasant anyhow, well,
then I prefer the other.

—But never this, this life now, here, the real one . . .?

—No, I suppose not. But I can't *imagine* it any different from the way it is—I can only *fantasy* a different life,
my old life, with you, or as someone else altogether,
someone created by the public, as a kind of community
effort, you know . . . ? That's how bitter *I* am.

(*Both Egress and Naomi Ruth break into nervous
laughter.*)

—Well, I don't suppose we should have breakfast
together, do you? The pain. . . .

—We might be seen by a columnist, you know. The Green Tulip Room is not exactly your cozy, little, out-of-the-way café. We don't need any more gossip than we've already endured, do we, now? As it is, by the time you get back to your apartment, or wherever you're living now, you'll flip on the radio or TV, only to hear that Egress and Naomi Ruth "accidentally" met in the lobby of the Plaza outside the Green Tulip Room, spoke quietly together for a few moments, and then went their separate ways, etc. Where *are* you living now, incidentally? In the city?

—Yes. As a matter of fact, I've been staying right here at the Plaza—all winter.

—Amazing.

—Yes.

—Yes, well, good-bye, now. . . . It's been . . . *odd*.

—*Hasn't* it! But pleasant, too. We'll have to do it again, sometime. . . .

—Yes. Well, good-bye.

—Good-bye.

—Good-bye.

—Yes. Bye.

—Bye.

—So long.

—*Ciao*.

—*Ciao*.

—Tra.

—La.

7.

(At the Party)

THEY SPOTTED EACH OTHER AT THE SAME INSTANT ON opposite sides of the crowded, smoke-draped room and made their respective ways through the crowd, holding their cocktail glasses over their heads so as not to spill, excusing themselves with careful graciousness as they stepped on toes, crunched corsages, bumped breasts, kicked canes, until they finally were together, breathless, in the center of the room, light peck on the cheek, sip from the drink as eyes appraise each other's bodies, faces, clothes, cigarettes lit, puffing, smiling nod to acquaintance nearby, appreciative and only slightly critical analysis of the posh apartment's décor, and, at last,

—Well, I didn't expect to run into *you* here! Naomi Ruth said in a hard but gay voice.

—And I didn't expect to run into you *here!* Egress countered.

—Jesus, Egress, we can't seem to say anything new to one another, can we?

—Not at this level, m'love. There's lots we could say if we weren't so obsessively intent on discussing our failed marriage every time we happened to meet.

—I know, she said sadly.

—Too bad we can't fuck, he said. —By God, *then* we'd have something new to talk about!

—Yes.

—I know.

—Yes.

—Um. Well, it's been "real," as they say. . . .

—Yes. Did you come alone? she asked him.

—Oh, no, no, no. No, I came with a "friend."

—Yes, she said, believing him. —The dancer. The young Russian girl. I remember.

—You alone? he queried idly.

—No, no. No, I'm not. Well, good-bye, Egress, she said hurriedly and started to pull away from the center of the room.

—Good-bye! he called after her.

A friend, a man obviously attracted to Naomi Ruth's not inconsiderable beauty, happened to be standing just behind Egress, and, recognizing his bluff voice, punched him affectionately on the shoulder, and said to him, —Hey, ol' buddy, who's that fine-looking woman you were just propositioning?

—Oh, that's just . . . that's my ex-wife.

—You sound regretful, ol' buddy.

—Naw. Not regretful. The wages of sin, you know. Wistful, though . . . and something else. But not regretful.

8.

(At the Casino)

—STAY CLOSE, M'LOVE. I STARTED WINNING THE SECOND you entered the room, and I'll have to quit if you leave.

—Do you think there are some sort of house rules against . . . ?

—Against what? Luck?

—I thought it was slightly more than that, luck. I mean, the way you carried on. . . .

—Well, it is more than luck, of course, but we don't want *them* to know it, because, yes, there is a house rule against magic, another against divine intervention, a third against astral projection, and so on. Your usual house rules.

—Which one are *we* breaking, confidentially? Whisper it.

He whispered into her diamond-encrusted ear. She shuddered down into her furs. He turned back to the table and continued winning.

It was quite a night, for both of them. They had such a good time together that on several occasions, half a dozen, at least, the pain brought one or the other of them to his knees. They were almost relieved when it was over and they could go back to their respective hotels along the Strip.

9.

(At the Bank)

—MAKING A DEPOSIT OR WITHDRAWAL? SHE ASKED HIM.

—Oh! I almost didn't recognize you in that business suit. A withdrawal, as it happens. What about you?

—Deposit.

—Neat, he said appreciatively.

—What?

—Oh, you know, the balance of payments, as it were. It's almost cosmic. I *love* analogies, as you well know, he reminded her gently.

—I don't need to be reminded, she informed him.

—Yes, I remember your telling me that, too. And just about everything else we say to each other as well.

—It's not exactly an opportunity for adventure, is it, being one of a pair of parallel lines? We stayed together too long, Egress, she reminded him again.

—Yes, I know, I know. I've been thinking about that a lot lately. Remembering it, I mean.

—What's the solution?

—Infinity, he laughed.

—No, be serious, Egress.

—I am, I am. We're a pair of parallel lines, you said it yourself, and if that's become a problem, as it most evidently has, then the only solution is "infinity," which is where they meet, finally.

—Or diverge.

—Right, or diverge. Of course. But we're not Greeks, nor were we meant to be, so we ought to be careful not to get our ethics mixed up with our mathematics. We're neither of us skilled enough a mathematician to accomplish it with anything like grace or good feeling.

—Don't worry about me, she said. —You're the one who loves analogy, remember?

—Yes, yes, of course. But you're the one who brought the parallel lines into this, which I've merely accepted as an indication of how you perceive our lives, past, present, and, presumably, future.

—I can't stand this quarreling. It's all so familiar to me, she exclaimed. —So *déjà-vu*. Good-bye, she said to him, and hurried from the bank.

He finished his transaction with the teller and left also, feeling no stranger to his anger with himself, even taking perverse pleasure from the familiarity.

10.

(In the Cocktail Lounge)

—H'LO AGAIN.

—Again. And again. And again. And again. And again. And again. And again. And again. And again. And again. And again.

—Been here awhile, eh?

—The better part of a season, I'd say. I thought I'd found a place you'd not found and wouldn't. But here you are. I see I should've kept moving, should've kept taking those chances instead of this one. . . .

—I'm sorry.

—*Don't* be! No, it's not *your* fault! None of it. Not a bit.

—I've changed.

—I know it. I can tell that. I know you've changed. Trouble is, I've changed too. And you know where that puts us? I'll tell you where it puts us! It puts us right back where we started. What we've got to do is change, all right, but only one of us at a time!

—Right. Well, don't let me interrupt you. Bye.

—Yeah. G'bye. Too bad for the bartender, though.

—Why?

—Wal, y'see, he just lost *two* customers. A "regular" and a "potential."

—Oh, I know. Well, don't worry, someone else will take our places, I'm sure.

—Yeah, sure, the world is full of people running away from each other.

—Right. Bye.

—G'bye.

11.

(At the Hospital)

—ARE YOU A PATIENT?
  —Here for tests.
  —Really? Anything wrong?
  —No, I'm sure it's nothing at all. A little innocuous bleeding. A lump or two, shortness of breath. But still, one has to treat these things as if they were serious. . .
  —I know.
  —What about you?
  —The same. Tests, X-rays.
  —Nothing serious, I hope?
  —Not really. A cough, occasional pain, a cut on my wrist that won't heal properly . . . Probably coincidence.
  —Of course. Like our checking in here at the same time, eh?
  —Yes, sure. Just like that.

12.

(At the Opera)

—No?
  —No.
  —Right.
  —Right?

About the Author

Russell Banks is the author of THE BOOK OF JAMAICA, FAMILY LIFE, SEARCHING FOR SURVIVORS, HAMILTON STARK, THE NEW WORLD, TRAILER-PARK, THE RELATION OF MY IMPRISONMENT, CONTINENTAL DRIFT, and SUCCESS STORIES. He has won Guggenheim and National Endowment for the Arts fellowships, the St. Lawrence Award for Fiction, and Fels, O. Henry, and Best American Short Story awards. He lives in New York City.

Compelling Contemporary Fiction

by RUSSELL BANKS

Available at your bookstore or use this coupon.

___CONTINENTAL DRIFT   33021   4.95

 BALLANTINE MAIL SALES
Dept. TA, 201 E. 50th St., New York, N.Y. 10022

Please send me the BALLANTINE or DEL REY BOOKS I have checked above. I am enclosing $...............(add $2.00 to cover postage and handling for the first book and 50¢ each additional book). Send check or money order—no cash or C.O.D.'s please. Prices are subject to change without notice. Valid in U.S. only. All orders are subject to availability of books.

Name_____

Address_____

City_____State_____Zip Code_____

Allow at least 4 weeks for delivery.   **TA-146**